Amulet Books
New York

Cataloging-in-Publication Data has been applied for and may be obtained from the Library of Congress.

ISBN 978-1-4197-3693-3

Text copyright © 2020 Heidi Lang
Book design by Siobhán Gallagher

Printed and bound in U.S.A.
10 9 8 7 6 5 4 3 2 1

Amulet Books are available at special discounts when purchased in quantity for premiums and promotions as well as fundraising or educational use. Special editions can also be created to specification. For details, contact specialsales@abramsbooks.com or the address below.

ABRAMS The Art of Books
195 Broadway, New York, NY 10007
abramsbooks.com

For my cousin Christy Buncic, the original "Claire-bear"
and one of the best people I know

Never let the facts get in the way of a good story.

—Old Irish Proverb

CHAPTER 1

Claire no longer believed her dad. Oh, she used to. No matter how wildly inventive his story, there was a time when she always fell for it. Like when she was six, and he'd convinced her there was a spaceship buried in their backyard. She'd dug for hours in the hot sun, dug until her fingers were more blister than skin. And when her shovel had scraped against metal buried deep beneath the soil, she'd been so sure she was about to discover a real UFO. Until she'd dug a little further and realized it was only their sewer. She'd thrown down her shovel in disgust, while her dad laughed and said, "Nice job, Claire-bear. I needed to check on that."

The next year, he'd told her that their downstairs was haunted, and she'd avoided it for months, terrified of the banging and scraping noises that came echoing through the floor. Until the day she'd decided that seven was too old to be scared of ghosts, and she'd forced herself to creep silently down, one careful step at a time. Instead of a poltergeist, she'd caught her dad converting a section of the basement into a new bedroom for her. "So you won't have to share a room with your brother much longer," he'd explained, followed by a grand, arms-out-wide gesture, his fingers wiggling. "Surprise!"

After that, Claire should have known better, but at eight, she still believed in the troll kingdom that lurked beneath their world, and the cunning and vicious king who ruled over the other trolls with a moss-covered fist. "You hear that?" her dad would say whenever the pipes in the house gurgled. "That's one of King Mossofras's snipes traveling back to its master." He loved telling stories like that, stories about the snipes who spied, and the trolls who prowled, and the magic hidden just below the surface. But his favorite troll story to tell was the one about Claire's mother, and how he had rescued her from King Mossofras and his Kingdom Below long before Claire was born.

"That crafty old king was a master of riddles, but we tricked him," her dad would say. "Or . . . we thought we did. Turns out you can't trick the troll king forever." He claimed that after Claire's brother, Patrick, was born, when Claire was four years old, the king had stolen their mother back. And when Claire was six, and seven, and even eight, that story had made perfect sense. But she'd always assumed her mother would come back someday, reappearing in their lives like a fairy-tale princess. So by nine—even though she still hopped out of the tub first before pulling the drain so the snipes couldn't grab her with their rubbery arms—she wasn't as satisfied with her dad's explanation about her mom anymore.

She began asking her dad where her mom *really* was, until finally he admitted her mom had once again escaped the troll kingdom, this time without his help. "She's a pilot now on the world's fastest jet," he'd said, adding that it was so fast it could travel from one side of the world to the next in a heartbeat. Claire barely remembered her mother, but in her imagination, she pictured the woman from the wedding photo her dad kept framed in the living room, only instead of a white dress and tiara, she wore goggles and a leather jacket, and she saw the whole world beneath her as one giant bluish-white blur. But eventually Claire got tired of that story, too, and began asking again and again, until her dad's story changed.

Now her mother was a curse breaker, working deep beneath the catacombs of Paris. Or a scientist at a crayon factory, trying to invent a new color. Or, finally, a secret agent, deep undercover in the wilds of the African Sahara. "She's just infiltrated a pride of lions," he had said, dropping his voice and leaning in close, like he was sharing classified information. And Claire had realized that it didn't matter where her mother actually was; her dad was never going to tell her. Maybe he didn't know, either. So, at ten, she tried another question: "Why doesn't she ever call?"

Instead of launching immediately into an answer like he usually did, her dad had hesitated. For one second, Claire felt like she was six years old again, her shovel scraping at the dirt, about to uncover some truth hidden beneath. But then her dad had smiled and said it was because her mom had been trapped in an invisible box by a troupe of mimes. "Can't talk, you see," he'd explained, shaking his head. It was then Claire knew that if she wanted the truth, she'd need to find it herself.

So the next year, when she was eleven, that's exactly what she did.

And after that, she never trusted another one of her dad's stories.

The problem was that sometimes, when he sounded like he *must* be lying, he wasn't.

Like right now.

"You're *not* serious," Claire said.

"I'm never serious," her dad said. "Except right now." And he gave her *the smile*.

People claimed that smiles were contagious, but her dad's smile didn't so much spread as steamroll everyone around it until they either joined in on the fun or got out of the way. Claire had learned there was no reasoning with a smile like that. Still, she tried.

"Dad, we can't move into a van."

"And why not?"

"Because it's...it's just...it's..." Claire floundered. This was the problem with her dad's ideas. His stories. His *everything*. He acted like it would be perfectly reasonable to, say, climb a tree in order to touch the moon. Then, the next thing you knew, you were reaching for the stars. Which was all well and good until those branches broke beneath you.

And Claire was tired of falling. "No," she said. "Just, no."

"Ooh, cool van, Dad!" Her brother, Patrick, skidded to a halt next to them, skinny arms pinwheeling. Like their dad, Patrick always seemed to have too much energy for his small body to contain. With his curly white-blond hair and those huge blue eyes, he looked like a little cherub. Claire had darker blond hair that hung limp and straight to her shoulders, and when she smiled, which wasn't often, she didn't have the dimples her brother and father had, and no one felt the need to join in or move out of the way.

"Dad thinks we're going to live in that," she told Patrick.

"What, in the van?" Patrick turned his wide eyes on her. "All three of us?"

"Hashtag vanlife, eh?" her dad said.

"Dad, for the last time, you don't *say* hashtag," Claire said. "And you know those videos and pictures are highly staged, right? No one is really that comfortable in a van."

"What? Staged? On the internet?" Her dad widened his own blue eyes, his glasses magnifying them until they were painful to look at. "If you can't trust the internet, what can you trust?"

"Ha ha, so funny. So very funny."

"I thought so." He grinned.

Claire shook her head, focusing again on the huge white monstrosity lurking in their driveway. Practically dwarfing their small house. What was her dad thinking, getting a van like that, threatening to pack them into it? And ... wait a second. She frowned at the van, studying the fancy emblem on the back. It looked expensive. Oh, it wasn't new; she could see a little bit of rust around the wheel wells and along the dent in the side panel. And there were a few other dents near the top where someone had obviously backed it into a spot too low for it. But still. Her dad couldn't afford something like this.

He patted the side of the van affectionately. "She's a beaut, isn't she?"

"Where did you get it?" Claire asked.

"Her."

"That's not a person, Dad. It's an object."

"*She* is much more than an object, my dear child. My poor, confused offspring. She is a vehicle of adventure."

Claire's stomach dropped. Whenever her dad used the a-word, she knew they were in trouble. It meant he was invested. It meant he had *plans*.

"Where did you get her, Dad?" Patrick asked. Eagerness practically radiated off of him in waves. He'd picked up on the a-word, too, only he didn't seem to realize that any adventure of their father's would be no good for either of them. Claire fought the urge to either pat her innocent little brother on his curly head or throttle him, because really? He should know better by now.

"Ah, that's an interesting story." Her dad leaned back against the van and crossed his arms. "Would you believe me if I said—"

"No," Claire said shortly.

He raised his eyebrows. "I haven't even started yet."

"Doesn't matter. Any time you say, 'That's an interesting story,' I know it's just that. A story."

"So young and so cynical," he sighed.

"And whose fault is that?"

"I'd believe you, Dad," Patrick chimed in. He hopped from foot to foot. "You can tell me."

Their dad grinned. "Well, you know our old family legend?"

"Which one?" Claire asked. "The one about your grandfather and his deal with the troll king? Or your sister and how she discovered the fifth dimension? Or—"

"None of those. I'm talking older than us, older than my sister. Older, even, than my grandfather. No, my grandfather's . . . grandfather, in fact. Good ole Wrong Way Jacobus."

"Wrong Way Jacobus?" Patrick stopped hopping. "Was that really his name?"

"Well, it became his name, son. Because of what he did."

"And what did he do?" Patrick asked.

"Ah, now that is an even more interesting story."

Claire groaned. Clearly her dad wasn't in the mood to give them real answers. But for some reason, she stayed. Not because she cared about her dad's newest ridiculous story. But just . . . because.

Their dad beamed at them and began his tale.

CHAPTER 2

Before he was 'Wrong Way,' your great-grandfather—"

"Don't you mean great-great-great-grandfather?" Claire interrupted. "I mean, if he's your grandfather's grandfather, then—"

"Are you telling this story, or am I?"

"I'm just trying to keep it accurate." Claire shook her head. "Which is like trying to towel off in a monsoon."

"Ooh, good one, Claire," Patrick whispered.

"Hmm." Their dad made his thinking face, forehead scrunched, mouth puckered like he was sucking on something. "That was pretty good, actually."

Claire tried not to feel proud, but her lips curled upward ever so slightly before she could stop them.

"So. Your great-great-great-grandfather, before the events of this tale, was named Edgar Jacobus. He lived in a tiny, picturesque village in France, where he spent his days working in a bakery, and where it's said he had invented a crust so hard, people built houses out of it. But only if they wanted a house that could last forever.

"In fact, that was the only kind of bread he could make. Still, Edgar was happy in his village and at his job. He never thought of leaving, although some nights he lay awake in his narrow bed tucked in his narrow room and wondered..."

"Wondered what, Dad?" Patrick asked, rapt, and Claire knew her brother had slipped beneath their father's spell.

Their dad's smile was wistful. "That most persistent, eternal question: what else is there?" He shifted his weight, the van creaking behind him. "And then one day, the owner of the bakery, who was Edgar's very own uncle, and your great-great-great-great-uncle—I'm sure Claire will correct me if I'm wrong on that—"

But Claire was lost now, too, the story forming inside her mind, the way her dad's stories always seemed to, the words reaching deep inside her, reaching that place she kept trying to leave behind.

"Well, he pulled Edgar aside, and everything changed..."

"Edgar, my dear, dear boy. You are my sister's only son, and I love you as if you were my own child. In fact, I love you more than all the grapes in my vineyard, and you know how I love those grapes."

"I know," Edgar said. He stood taller.

"And I love you more than the entire flock of sheep in my beautiful fields, and you know how I love those sheep. *And* those fields."

"I know." Edgar puffed out his chest.

"But, I do not love you more than this bakery, and unfortunately, you are terrible for business."

Edgar deflated. "What? Terrible?"

"Oh, my dear boy, you have no idea. I've thought of sacking you so many times. So many times! But greater still than my love for you is my fear of my sister."

"But, terrible?" Edgar couldn't believe it. "People come from miles away for my bread!"

"Only when they are in need of weapons. Or building supplies. Never for eating."

"But—"

"Poor Madam Lamar cracked two teeth! And she's the third one this week. No, my dear boy, I can't have you in my shop. Not for another moment. It has become impossible." His expression had grown harder than any bread, even one of Edgar's own creations, and Edgar knew there would be no moving him.

So, armed only with two baguettes and a spare pair of clothes, Edgar left. He allowed himself one last look at his tiny cottage, tucked behind the bakery. The fields around it weren't quite as green as he'd always thought, the sheep not as fluffy, and some of the grapes were shriveled and dry.

When he turned away, he felt a weight lifting from his shoulders. If he stayed, he knew what his life would be. Day in and day out, unchanging. But out there, anything could be waiting for him.

Including the answer to that persistent, eternal question.

So he said good-bye in his heart to the life he'd known, and set out on the open road, never to return. And thus began the very first Jacobus Grand Adventure.

Claire blinked. Her dad had gone quiet. Had *been* quiet, in fact, for a good minute, his eyes fixed on their small house. For the first time, Claire noticed the shadows pooling under those eyes, the way the lines in his face seemed deeper, like someone had traced them with a thick black pen. He looked . . . old. Old and tired.

"Dad?" she asked.

He glanced down at her and smiled. "Claire-bear?"

Her dad was just fine. Claire scowled.

"Watch it," he warned, "or your face will freeze like that. Then we'd be forced to track down a witch to fix you back up, and they're hard to find. Impossible, even." He leaned down. "You've seen your aunt Jan's face."

Yep, definitely fine. "That's mean," Claire said. "No wonder she doesn't like to visit us anymore." Claire couldn't remember the last time her aunt had come out to see them.

Her dad winced. "Yes. Well. She's a busy woman."

"What about the rest of Wrong Way's story?" Patrick asked. "Where did he go?"

"I'm saving the rest for later."

"Aww," Patrick whined.

Their dad pushed away from the van and ruffled Patrick's curls. "It'll be a story for the road, eh? Now, who wants to help me fix this baby up? The sooner she's ready, the sooner we can hit that dusty horizon."

"Ugh, count me out." Claire turned away, then hesitated. Her dad never liked to give the whole story at once, and not just when he was spinning a wild tale. She realized there was also a lot he hadn't explained about this new venture of his. "Dad..." she said slowly, carefully, "where are we going in the van?"

"Wherever the road takes us!" He grinned.

"Okay. Not helpful." Claire sighed. "Can you at least tell me how long we'll be in the van, then? I had plans with Ronnie this summer."

His grin slipped. "Er, yes. Well. Actually, that's something I wanted to talk to you about." He looked at Patrick, then back at Claire. "Both of you."

CHAPTER 3

Ronnie picked up on the first ring. "Claire! What's—"

"My dad bought a van there's no way he could afford and it's probably stolen and now he wants us to live in it," Claire said in a rush.

Silence.

"Hello?" Claire pressed the phone harder into her ear. "Did you hear me? Why aren't you talking?"

"I was giving your words a little bit of space. You know, since you didn't."

"Ronnie! This is no time for space!" Claire ground her teeth.

"There's always time for space," Ronnie said in that slow, deep drawl of hers, like she had all the time in the world and nothing could rush her. When Claire met Ronnie back in kindergarten, she'd fallen in love with that voice. It had reminded Claire of the rolling waves of nearby Lake

Huron, patient and endless, and she'd decided then and there that Ronnie would be her best friend forever.

But today, that particular Ronnie quality wasn't so admirable. Today, it was simply irritating. "Look, can we leave space behind for a minute?" Claire asked. "My dad. Bought. A van."

"I guess that is pretty surprising."

"Thank you." Claire shifted on her bed, her anger redirecting back toward her dad. "Hashtag vanlife. Can you even believe it?"

"Hashtag vanlife?" Ronnie said.

"It's this thing online where people live in their vans and then post pictures of all their adventures. My dad is totally hooked."

"This is exactly why old people should stay off the internet. Gives them ideas." *Click-click. Click-click.*

"Ronnie," Claire sighed. "Are you tapping a pen against your teeth again?"

Silence.

"You know what your mom would say."

Ronnie's mother had spent a fortune on braces for Ronnie and was very protective of her teeth. Ronnie wasn't allowed to eat or drink anything with more than five grams of sugar in it, which was actually harder than Claire would have thought. And nothing chewy. Ever. Pen tapping? A definite no.

Click-click-click.

"Ronnie," Claire warned.

"It's not me this time! I put my pen down."

"Really?" Claire listened. The clicking stopped, then started again, along with, "Mike, is that you?" No response. "Mike!"

"Alright, alright." Mike laughed. "It's me. What gave me away?"

"You're a mouth breather," Claire said. "We could hear you a mile away."

"No, you couldn't. I've been listening the whole time," he crowed.

"Ronnie," Claire said sharply. It was always Ronnie's job to check the phone lines before they started talking. Otherwise her younger brother, Mike, would lurk there, eavesdropping on everything. Because, like Claire, Ronnie was stuck using a landline. Unlike Claire, it had nothing to do with finances.

"As you'll recall, *someone* refused to allow me any space, so I couldn't check," Ronnie said. "Besides, Mike's gotten sneakier about it."

"Yeah, I have," Mike said.

"Don't sound so smug," Ronnie said. "We all know why you keep doing this."

"Why?" Claire asked.

"Oh, you know, because he has a huge crush on you."

"What? No, I don't!"

"Whatever, Mike. Claire already knows."

"But I don't!"

Ronnie laughed, and a second later there was a soft *click*. "And that takes care of that," she chortled.

Claire's face felt too hot, the phone sticking to her skin. "He doesn't really, does he?" she asked. A boy had never had a crush on her before. Even if it *was* just Mike. He was only a year younger than Ronnie, but still, that was way, way too young. He'd barely turned eleven. It would be too weird.

"Nah, I was just trying to get him to hang up. Now, about this van."

"The van. Right. Yes." Claire coughed.

"So, give me the details. How long are you gone for? You'll be back for my birthday, right?"

All thoughts of crushes vanished beneath the weight of the answer. "No," Claire said slowly. "I'll be missing your birthday this summer." She put a hand against her chest, pressing against her heart. She had to tell Ronnie all of it. "I'll be missing all of them."

"*What?*"

"Dad's planning on selling our house once the van's converted. He thinks it'll be the grandest adventure yet, the three of us living in a van."

"Forever?" Ronnie asked, and for once she sounded shocked. Like maybe time had sped up on her. "Like, permanently?"

"I don't think forever forever," Claire admitted. "He hasn't said as much, but I'm assuming eventually we'll stop traveling and live somewhere."

"But not here."

"No. I mean, he hasn't been able to get a new job since he got laid off, and that was months ago." Actually, it was almost a year ago, but she didn't really want to talk about that with Ronnie. Ronnie's mother taught physics at the local university, and her dad did some sort of IT job. They claimed they weren't rich, but compared to Claire's family, Ronnie might as well have been the Princess of Wales.

"I thought he was working?"

Claire flopped onto her bed and stared at her ceiling. Her dad had painted it a deep purplish blue years ago and helped her paste glow-in-the-dark stars on it. She remembered him holding her up so she could press the small shapes into the ceiling herself, both of them checking and rechecking the star chart they'd made earlier that week.

She turned on her side so she wouldn't have to look at it anymore. "He's gotten a few contract positions," she said, "but nothing permanent. Nothing with benefits." Her dad had struggled to hold on to a full-time job ever since the steel mill closed a few years ago.

He'd once described working in their city of Marsdale, Michigan, as standing on the edge of the beach. The ground would feel solid beneath your feet, you'd get your toes pressed in firmly, and then one little wave would suck that sand right out from under you. If that wave didn't get you, the next would, or the next, and eventually you'd be up to your ankles in water and looking for another job again.

Ronnie didn't answer, and beneath the heavy silence that followed were the distinctive sounds of a mouth breather.

"Mike?" Claire said. "You're eavesdropping again, aren't you?"

"No," Mike said.

"Mike," Ronnie sighed. "Hang. Up. The. Phone."

"You need me," Mike said.

"We need you?" Ronnie said. "I suppose there's a first time for everything."

"Claire, your dad's gone full bohemian," Mike continued, ignoring his sister. "I was afraid this might happen."

"Full bohemian?" Ronnie snorted.

"You saw this coming?" Claire added.

"Oh, definitely. Your dad has always had the soul of a true vagabond. But don't worry. We'll stop him. Right, Ronnie?"

"Um, sure..."

"How?" Claire asked.

"Wait right there. We're coming over."

CHAPTER 4

The van towered over Claire as she approached, like some kind of metal beast ready to swallow her whole. When she realized her dad would love that description, she immediately discarded it.

"Dad?" she called over the thrumming bassline of his newest band obsession. She poked her head through the open side door.

Her dad and Patrick were crouched beside a bucket full of suds, their pants rolled up, both of them scrubbing at the rubber flooring and belting the chorus together. Claire watched them for almost a minute, her heart aching. She used to embrace her dad's Grand Adventures, too. *Starlit skies and spaceships and anything is possible . . .*

Her dad looked up. "Claire-bear! Come to join us?"

She took a step back. "No. Just, uh, Mike and Ronnie are coming over."

"Awesome possum."

Claire winced.

"Can you take our picture?" Patrick asked. "For our hashtag vanlife project?"

"What?" Claire shook her head. "Oh, Patrick, not you, too."

"Please? Please?" Patrick had soap in his hair and a smear of dirt down the left side of his face. It would make a pretty cute picture actually, especially with the two of them wearing matching plaid shirts.

"Fine," Claire sighed. She looked around for her dad's phone but didn't see it.

"It's right there," he told her, pointing with one soapy finger to a cell phone perched precariously on the outer step of the van. "I got a new one for the trip."

"It's about time," Claire muttered. He'd hung on to his old flip phone forever. She turned on the screen, and a text message icon flashed in the corner from an unknown number. All Claire could read was the start of the message:

The kids are def going to be a problem—no openings here for them, but check w/Jul...

Her finger hovered over it. The kids? That didn't mean her and Patrick...did it? And no openings for them...that almost sounded like—

"Everything okay?" her dad asked, and she tapped the camera icon instead, leaving the message untouched.

"Aside from the fact that you think we're going to live in a vehicle—"

"We *are* going to live in a vehicle."

"—everything's just peachy. Smile."

"Hashtag, hashtag!" Patrick chirped as Claire snapped their pic.

Their dad wiped his hands on his shirt and took the phone from her. "Look at those handsome fellas, eh?" He showed Patrick their pic, then frowned. "A message?" A second later his frown deepened, turning into an ugly scowl, the same kind of look he wore that one time Mr. Truxel showed up with all those forms from the bank.

"Dad says we're going to the Studebaker Museum in Indiana first so we can see all the old carriages. You know, before there were cars." Patrick was practically bouncing, he was so excited. "Right, Dad?"

Their dad shook his head, his thumbs moving rapidly as he typed some response. Still scowling, he looked up, his eyes widening as he caught both kids staring at him.

"Studebaker?" Patrick asked.

"Everything okay?" Claire added.

"Oh, absolutely." The scowl vanished beneath another bright smile. "But I'm wondering, now, if we shouldn't just skip Indiana and go straight to Ohio." He glanced back at his phone once, his smile flickering, before he shoved it away in his back pocket.

"No museum?" Claire raised her eyebrows. Her dad loved museums. He tried dragging her and Patrick into them any chance he got, so for him to decide to skip one when he'd actually gotten Patrick's vote to go was very unlike him.

"Oh, there will be plenty more museums in Ohio, I'm sure."

"But, Dad—" Patrick started.

"No, west is the wrong direction. We must go east. East, my son!"

Patrick tilted his head, considering. "What's east?"

"That's what we're going to find out. Now, who can tell me what three things make up your typical troll?"

"Aww, that's easy. They are," Patrick stuck his finger in the air, flinging droplets of soapy water, "rocks!" Another finger up. "Moss!" He grinned and threw up a third finger. "And pure, cold spite," he and their dad said together.

"Did someone mention spite?" Ronnie rolled up on her bicycle, her brown hair in braided pigtails trailing beneath her bright red helmet. "Hey there, Scotland."

"Veronica!" Claire's dad hopped out of the van and gave Ronnie a fist bump. "And how is my second-favorite girl?"

"Claire's still the favorite, huh?" Ronnie said.

"Always." He nudged Claire in the shoulder.

"I'm so honored," Claire muttered, even as she tried not to be.

"So, you got yourself a van," Ronnie said.

"I sure did! She's a beaut, too, eh?"

"Hey, you jerk!" Mike yelled.

"Dang. He caught up." Ronnie took off her helmet and hung it on her bike handle.

"What did you do?" Claire whispered.

"Nothing," Ronnie said, but she was doing that thing with her face she always did when she was lying. Claire could never figure out exactly what it was, something about how she held her jaw. And all of a sudden it hit her: if they moved, she might never see Ronnie's lying face again.

She wanted to cry.

She wanted to kick this stupid van.

Mike ran up the driveway, then bent over and put his hands on his legs, panting. His shirt was soaked through with sweat, his dark hair sticking out in all directions.

"Nice afternoon for a run, eh?" Claire's dad said.

"My bike tires were flat," Mike wheezed. He glared at Ronnie. "I *told* you so."

"So, what? I was supposed to let you use my bike?"

"You're a better runner than I am."

Ronnie smirked. "That's definitely true."

"You weren't that far behind her," Claire pointed out.

Ronnie shot her The Look. It was a look forged through years of sleepovers and shared secrets and it meant one thing: you are breaking a core rule. Right now, Claire was breaking the rule of never siding with Mike against Ronnie. Ever.

Claire could feel her face heating. "I was just saying, he ran pretty fast. You know, for him."

"Hmm," Ronnie said.

"So, Scottie." Mike straightened, pushed his hair back, and stuck his scrawny chest out. "You're planning on ripping your family away, stuffing them inside this tiny box on wheels, and taking off for parts unknown. Is that about right?"

Scottie laughed. "You turn a phrase better than anyone I know."

"Thanks." Mike beamed.

"My dad also says things like 'awesome possum,' so I wouldn't be too proud of that compliment," Claire said.

"You're saying I should consider the source?" Mike asked, still grinning.

Claire's stomach tightened, and for some reason she couldn't look away. He had a nice smile, actually. It made the corners of his eyes crinkle. *He has a huge crush on you...*

Claire turned away, then froze.

Ronnie was staring straight at her, brown eyes narrowed. "Hmm," she repeated, and it felt like an entire story was hidden within that one sound. Claire was actually relieved when her dad interrupted.

"So, whattaya think?" He knocked on the side of the van with his fist.

"This is a really cool van." Mike trailed one hand along the side as he circled it.

Ronnie cleared her throat. "Are you sure about that, Mike?"

"I like the tall roof so you can stand inside it. A Sprinter crew van, I see. Very nice. Sleek. Like a shark."

Claire's dad practically glowed with pride. "Thanks, Mike. That means a lot, coming from a smart young man like yourself."

Mike's face twitched. He *was* smart. So smart he'd been moved up two grades, which he used to mention whenever he got a chance. He knew it bugged Ronnie that he was a year younger and a grade ahead. But something had happened during this past school year. Ronnie had told Claire that a month into it, he'd tried to get moved back down into a lower grade. Their mother had refused to even consider it.

These days, he never bragged about being smart. He never bragged about anything, really.

He scrubbed a hand over his face, and it was like he was putting on a mask, all his earlier approval vanishing beneath it. "I see you chose the 144-inch model, though. Honestly, that seems a little too short for converting into a home. Not like the 170."

"You know your stuff."

"I did my research," Mike said. "Naturally."

"When?" Claire whispered to Ronnie. She'd just told them about the van.

"You know Mike, he's always looking up weird stuff." Ronnie shrugged. "Probably looked up vans on a whim months ago."

"Well then *naturally*," Claire's dad continued, "I'm assuming you would have been pretty thorough in this research of yours."

"Of course," Mike said, standing up a little straighter.

"Then I'm sure you also know that the 144 will be much more fuel efficient, not to mention easier to park in cities."

"Okay, that's true," Mike said reluctantly. "But still. I don't see any way this can be a comfortable home for three people." He glanced at Claire. She gave him a subtle thumbs-up, and another smile flashed across his face. And Claire knew she'd miss that smile almost as much as she'd miss seeing Ronnie's lying face. Not that she'd ever tell Ronnie that.

Her dad sat down inside the open side door of the van. He nodded twice, like he was deep in thought. It was an act, though. Claire had seen him do the same thing a hundred times, pretending he might be swayed one way, when they all knew he'd already decided and wouldn't let a little thing like "reason" or "logic" stop him. "I'm not disagreeing with you," he said now. "It's definitely an unusual idea, and I don't blame you for not liking it. Not everyone recognizes when *unusual* is a good thing." He waited a beat. "But I think *you* do, Mike. You of all people would understand." He patted the space next to him.

"Mike," Claire said warningly.

"Hold up, Claire." Her dad raised a hand, palm out like a stop sign. "We're talking here."

Mike hesitated, then sat down. Uh-oh.

Claire and Ronnie exchanged looks.

"There's a reason I tried leaving him behind," Ronnie muttered.

Claire scowled as her dad turned back to Mike. "We're going with the minimalist model of conversion, so think more sleeping space and less...all those fancy bells and whistles. So plenty of space to make this into a comfortable enough home for us. My real question is...can I do it in fifteen days?"

"Fifteen days?" Mike's eyes widened.

"From van to home in fifteen days. That's the grand plan. Think it's possible?"

"It's going to be a stretch, Scottie," Mike said, all serious. Claire's dad had always insisted that Ronnie and Mike call him by his first name. He said his dad was Mr. Jacobus, and one in the family was quite enough. Claire used to think he just said that because he didn't want to feel old, but now, watching him with Mike, she suspected he had another motive.

Her dad was a master at figuring out what another person wanted, and making them think they could find it...

if they would *just*. Just dig that hole, hike that hill, climb that tree. Whatever it was, it would surely be a Grand Adventure. Just like it would surely benefit her dad. And Mike wanted friends. Claire knew that was the real reason he eavesdropped on his sister's conversations and followed them around. Calling her dad "Scottie" made Mike feel like they were buddies, which made him easier to manipulate.

"A stretch, eh?" Her dad made his thinking face, then nodded. "You know, I think you're right about that. Still, people told my great-great-grandfather," he winked at Claire, "good ole Wrong Way Jacobus, that he'd never be able to marry Evangeline Rose, on account of she was the most beautiful woman in the world. And also on account of how she'd attracted the attentions of the town marshal, a man with a quick gun hand and the blackest heart that side of the Mississippi."

"Did he marry her?" Mike asked.

"Now, that is an interesting story. I'd love to tell you all about it, but unfortunately I've got to get back to work on this here behemoth." He stood and stretched. "It'll be tough, an old back like mine. As you've pointed out, it's a real herculean task I've taken on here. I'm just glad I can count on my son to help me."

From inside the van, Patrick gave him a thumbs-up.

"Do you ... did you want more help?" Mike asked.

Claire watched her dad rub his chin, as if he were thinking deeply about that question. "I mean," he said slowly, like the idea had just occurred to him, "if I had another set of strong arms, well, that van would be as good as done. But I'd never dream of asking..."

And there it was. The hook, the line...

"I'll help! What do you need me to do first?"

And the sucker taking it.

"Mike!" Ronnie snapped, but her brother ignored her. Claire knew it was all over. Whatever plans Mike had made to help her stay had been steamrolled, another victim of her dad's persuasive enthusiasm. Claire knew she shouldn't be surprised, shouldn't feel betrayed.

Obviously, Mike didn't have such a crush on her after all.

Disappointment lined Claire's stomach, which was silly, really. She didn't like Mike anyhow. She didn't care if he liked her dad more than he liked her. *Most* people liked her dad more.

"Let's go, Claire." Ronnie took her arm and led her away. "He's lost to us."

They put Ronnie's bike in the backyard and headed inside. Claire's dad hadn't started using the air conditioner yet—he claimed Jacobuses thrived in the heat—which meant that sometimes entering their house felt like crawling inside a creature's sweaty mouth. Today was one of those times.

Luckily the basement was always a good ten degrees cooler than the rest of the house.

Claire sank gratefully onto her bedroom floor, digging her fingers into her worn beige carpet. Ronnie settled next to her. "My own brother," she muttered. "For someone so smart, sometimes that boy just doesn't have a clue."

"Well, we don't need him," Claire said.

"Right." Ronnie smiled. "We can come up with a plan on our own." And the way she said it, in her deep, slow voice, made Claire feel like maybe they really could stop this thing. "I brought my laptop so we could research the enemy."

"The enemy?"

Ronnie smirked. "Hashtag vanlife."

Claire groaned.

"What? We need to know what we're up against." Ronnie pulled her laptop out of her backpack, still all sleek and shiny, even though it was over a year old. Claire tried not to be jealous as her friend booted it up and attached her pocket Wi-Fi, since the Jacobuses did not have reliable internet. They settled in, clicking through Instagram pictures of happy couples wearing bathing suits and posing on their fancy van beds, the ocean in the background. Usually there was at least one dog.

"Maybe this will be your chance to get a pet," Ronnie said, clicking through a few more.

"Don't mention that to Patrick. He's been dying for a dog forever."

"You mean, furever?" Ronnie grinned.

Claire groaned. "Why do I even hang out with you?"

"You like a little irritation in your life."

"I *do* have my dad, you know."

"Point. I should go easier on you." Ronnie's grin slid away, her eyes gleaming as she went back to the pictures. She paused on one of a woman holding a surfboard and shielding her eyes from the sun. Behind her, a large bumper sticker on her van proclaimed, "Not all who wander are lost."

Claire reached over and gently closed the laptop.

"What?" Ronnie asked.

"You're getting caught up in it, aren't you? All this hashtag vanlife silliness."

Ronnie hesitated. "It does look a little...I don't know. Exciting."

Claire scowled. "It also looks fake. Do you see how 'happy' these people are? Barf. No one is that happy living in a vehicle."

"Just imagine it, though. You can pack up and leave and go anywhere you want. Just go."

Just go. And suddenly all Claire could picture was the photo of her mother she and Ronnie had found online last summer. Claire had given up asking her dad for answers by then, but she hadn't been ready to dig for them on her own just yet. Part of her had felt like her mom was more a character in a story than a real person, since all Claire had of her were a few hazy memories, a couple of old toys, and one or two photographs. But then one morning, she'd gone looking through a drawer for her favorite sketchbook and found a note from her mother. And beneath it, those papers... *divorce* papers.

The reality of her mother had slammed into her, and with it, the realization that her dad must have known the real reason her mom had left this whole time. He knew why, and he knew where she was, and even though Claire had asked a hundred times, he hadn't told her the truth, not once. And when he'd caught her hunched over those papers, crying, he hadn't said a word about them. She'd stopped caring about all his stupid stories after that, and the next weekend, she'd asked Ronnie if they could look up someone on Ronnie's brand-new laptop.

It didn't take Ronnie long to locate Claire's mother, living way out in northern California. Far, far away.

Claire closed her eyes, the photo they'd found burning beneath her lids. Her mom's hair had been cut much shorter than in her dad's wedding picture, the reddish blond dyed a warm chocolate, her face soft and full of laughter. Behind her, the walls gleamed white and the counters gleamed dark and everything looked new and expensive. A different person with a different life. The kind of person who *went* and never looked back.

Who would Claire become when she left here?

Claire wiped her face, her hand coming away damp.

"Oh, Claire." Ronnie put an arm around Claire's shoulder and hugged her awkwardly. Ronnie wasn't much of a hugger, but she tried, for Claire, and that just made Claire cry harder. "It'll be okay. You'll be back at the end of the summer."

"No, I won't," Claire sobbed. "I told you, Dad's planning on selling the house."

"He can try," Ronnie said dubiously. "Mom says all the houses here are going for pennies, practically. No one's buying. And once your dad gets tired of living in a van, he'll bring you back."

Claire hiccupped. "You think?"

"Oh, definitely," Ronnie said in her slow, confident voice. "After all, no one is that happy living in a vehicle, right?" She grinned. "He'll want to come home. Probably just in time for school."

Claire wanted to relax, but Ronnie didn't know her dad the way she did. His stories and Grand Adventures were always built in layers, like a fancy dessert. You had to dig your spoon in deeper to understand what was really buried there at the bottom of the glass.

Which meant this hashtag vanlife her dad had thrown himself into was probably about something else entirely.

Claire remembered that text message on her dad's phone and shivered. Maybe her mom wasn't the only one who wanted to leave them all behind.

CHAPTER 5

Every day for the next two weeks it was "van this" and "van that" while Claire's dad and brother and Mike all worked on the conversion. Sometimes a random neighbor would stop by and get roped into helping for a few hours, or one of Claire's dad's old friends might make the mistake of visiting and find themselves cutting wood and hammering nails, and whatever else they were up to out there. Once Claire had even caught Ronnie helping, but Claire had given her The Look and Ronnie had put down her paintbrush so fast it was like it had burned her. "Just trying to make it pretty for you," Ronnie had muttered. But after that, she stayed away from the van.

Even if Ronnie was convinced this would just be a long road trip, Claire was taking no chances. She knew how her dad's enthusiasm could spread like a disease. The only cure was to have limited contact and lots of scorn.

"It's called being homeless, Dad," she'd snapped the other day. She'd been rewarded by a flinch in his eyes, but then he'd brought out that ever-present smile, and the next day he'd hung up a sign over their kitchen table that read: I GO TO SLEEP IN MY VEHICLE AND I WAKE UP IN THE NEIGHBOR-HOOD OF MY CHOICE.

Clearly, he was doubling down. There'd be no stopping him. So Claire had reluctantly spent the next few days sorting and packing, and now she was theoretically ready to go.

She lay back on her bed and stared up at her painted sky, tracing the patterns of her glow-in-the-dark stars with her eyes. It had taken her and her dad forever to put them up, trying to keep those constellations as accurate as possible, her fingers still sore from digging in the yard the day before. They'd worked on her ceiling the morning after the great sewer-digging incident—she'd almost forgotten that.

A sudden memory hit her: her dad helping her press in the final star, then turning off the light so they could admire their work. How magical it had seemed to have the night sky trapped inside her room. "I'm sorry we didn't find a spaceship in the yard yesterday," her dad had whispered. "But maybe we'll find one tomorrow." Claire had spun slowly, illuminated by the glow of her new constellations, and she'd felt like maybe they would. Like anything might be possible.

The constellations blurred now in Claire's vision, and she ran a hand over her face quickly. It was stupid to cry.

Just because that feeling of anything was possible was as fake as the stars on her ceiling. The ceiling she might never see again, once they left here ...

"Claire-bear!"

Claire jerked upright just as her bedroom door flew open.

"Dad, jeez, a little privacy!"

"Sorry, sorry."

"Sorry people don't smile," Claire said. At least she didn't feel sad anymore, just irritated.

Patrick stuck his head in. "Party in Claire's room!"

"No!" Claire crossed her arms. "No party. Get out." Patrick liked to skulk around her room and go through her stuff. She'd caught him rifling through her desk drawers enough times that he was now permanently banished from her room.

"Why? It's not like you'll get privacy in Van-Helsing," Patrick pointed out.

Ugh. That was a good, and yet terrible, point. "Then you should let me enjoy it while I still can. And we are *not* calling the van that," she added.

"I thought you didn't care what we called it. Right, Dad? Claire said she didn't care."

"You did say that, Claire-bear."

Claire squeezed her hands into fists as tightly as possible and counted to five. When she let go, her fingers stayed

curled in place, slowly releasing like claws. It was a trick
Ronnie had taught her back in kindergarten, back when
Claire used to throw screaming tantrums. "By the time
your fingers straighten, you'll feel better," Ronnie had said.
Sometimes it worked.

"What's up with your claw hands?" Patrick asked.

Clearly this wouldn't be one of those times. Claire shook
out her hands, her fingers unfurling. "Nothing," she sighed.
"Why are you here?"

"Van's ready," her dad said. "Thought you might like to
take the grand tour." He bounced on the balls of his feet,
excitement radiating through every inch of him. Claire, on
the other hand, felt as if her feet were nailed to the ground,
and then stuffed full of lead. Still, she dragged herself out of
her room and followed her dad outside. Might as well get it
over with.

He pulled open the back doors and the side door and
threw his arms wide. "Ta-da!"

It looked ... sparse. There was the mattress, a twin, built
into a wooden stand that could fold in half and become a
couch.

"Look, the table pulls out from this wall," he said, rap-
ping the wood on the opposite wall proudly. "Your brother
sanded it, so make sure you compliment him when we use
it." He showed her the hammocks, both a painfully bright
red. "Cheery, right?" He'd nailed planks of wood lengthwise

across the van walls, and then added a small block of wood to the top of those planks to hold the hammocks in place. Claire would get a five-inch corridor of space between her hammock and Patrick's.

"Not a lot of space between us." Claire frowned.

"When you consider how much space total we have, five inches is really more like fifteen inches."

"Which would still not be a lot of space. When you consider that is the only space between me and my irritating brother."

"Well, honey, space is all relative."

"Tell that to Ronnie."

Her dad grinned, then continued with the tour, unde-terred. "The hammocks also slide out, so when my bed is folded up into a couch, we can lounge." He demonstrated. "See? Comfy cozy."

"Comfy cozy," Claire repeated flatly.

Next, he showed off the LED lights spaced around the sides, the cabinets up above, made from recycled wood pallets that had been sanded and stained and painted, the fan he'd installed himself in the roof. It looked more like a vent, like the fan in their bathroom. "Most expensive piece of equipment," he said, tapping it proudly. "But worth it. Every video I've seen says you've got to have this fan. See here? It can suck the air out of the van, or pull cooler air into it. Neat-o, right?"

"Please don't say neat-o."

"As a courtesy to my eldest daughter," he inclined his head, "I've stopped saying 'awesome possum,' because I hear that's 'uncool.'"

"So are air quotes, Dad."

"You're killin' me, Claire-bear. I'm running out of ways to express myself."

"That'll be the day." Claire shook her head. "So, where's the rest? The sink, the bathroom, the kitchen?"

"Ah. Yes. Well." He cleared his throat. "There's a panel that pulls out in the back. I installed legs that'll fold down, so when it's nice out, we can cook on that with our good ole camp stove."

"You mean the one that's a hundred years old and smells like gas?" Claire wrinkled her nose.

"That's the one!" He beamed. "I got us a good cooler. Here, see? With this cushion on it, so it doubles as a seat. And a seatbelt, so whoever isn't riding copilot is nice and safe back here." He touched the seatbelt proudly. "And this here." He tapped a narrow wooden bookshelf that had been nailed into the side of the van next to his bed. "The table will lay flat over this when I unfold it, but it can hold our water jugs, and there's this bucket here to drain the water into. I'll build us a sink later. Maybe. But this'll do for now. And look at all these pots and dishes stored nicely down here."

Claire looked around, her stomach sinking. It was less an RV and more just a van with a few additions. Nothing like the glossy vanlife photographs she and Ronnie had looked up. This would be one long, long summer. "And... the bathroom?" she prompted, hoping there was another compartment hidden away in there, somewhere, someway.

"Oh yeah. That. Well, I decided there was no point in putting in a toilet or shower. One, because this is the shorter version of the Sprinter, and honestly, space is a real issue. And—"

"Whoa, hold up," Claire said. "There's no bathroom?"

"Well... technically, no."

"It's better," Patrick said, hopping up into the van with them. "King Mossofras uses pipes to travel. This will make it harder for his snipes to catch us."

Claire rubbed her temple. "Patrick. Seriously. What's up with this sudden snipe obsession? And Dad, I am *not* living somewhere that doesn't have indoor plumbing. Period. I refuse."

"Hmm. That's gonna be tricky, Claire-bear, 'cause we're leaving in the morning, and this is all we've got."

Leaving in the morning.

The moment between one heartbeat and the next stretched for an eternity, stretched as if it might never end. Claire put a hand to her chest, took a breath. She'd known this was coming. Still. "Then I'll just have to stay here," she said.

"Can't. House is transferring to the new owners this week."

Claire gaped. "Wait, what?" She turned to look at their small house, with its striped green-and-white window awnings, the peeling yellow paint, the surprisingly large backyard. She'd been four when they'd moved in here, just before her mom had Patrick. And even if Claire could only barely remember when her mom disappeared, she still felt a twinge at the thought of leaving the last place they'd all been together, the place she'd had so many adventures. Pretending to be knights and dragons, climbing the fort her dad had built for her—and then torn down again, after she fell from the top and broke her wrist—painting that little fence in the corner with Patrick, the tiny sandpit they'd played in. All of it, gone.

And the stories. Her dad's stories of trolls and fairies and hidden kingdoms. Places where heroes dwelled, where little girls could defeat monsters as long as they followed the rule of threes, where magic made anything possible, and even missing mothers could be explained away, or forgotten. "You really sold the house?" she whispered. "Already?"

"I know this will be a big change." He put a hand on her shoulder and squeezed. "But it'll be a *good* change."

Claire blinked back tears. So much for Ronnie's confidence that the house wouldn't sell for a long time. They really *were* leaving, and even if her dad changed his mind on the road, they wouldn't have a house to come back to.

Patrick came over to her other side and slipped his small hand into hers, like he used to do when he was littler. He must be sad, too. This was the only home he'd ever known. He tugged on her hand. She leaned down, and he whispered in her ear, "If you wanted a toilet so much, maybe you should have helped with the van."

Claire yanked her hand away and stomped inside the house without another word. She'd have to call Ronnie, and tell her she'd been all wrong.

Everything was wrong.

CHAPTER 6

Tap-tap-tap. Tap-tap-tap.

Claire woke up slowly.

Tap-tap.

Her heart froze, all the blood pooling into one giant icy lump in her chest. She remembered her dad's stories about how, instead of fingernails, trolls had an extra finger bone sharpened to a fine point. How King Mossofras wanted revenge after her dad had stolen her mom out from under those pointed fingers of his years ago. And how Claire, young, innocent, would be easy prey if she wasn't careful.

"If you hear something scraping, scraping at your window in the dead of night, it's probably King Mossofras, searching for a weakness in my troll-repelling glass, so don't look. *Never* look. Because if he catches your gaze with his own, he'll be able to pull you to him and drag you belowground where you'll never see sunlight again . . ."

Claire squeezed her eyes shut. Just a story her dad had told her when she was little. She'd woken up crying every night for a week afterward, and her dad had never told that particular story again. But it still hovered there in her memory, and all it took was the smallest noise at night to send it careening back, the words as fresh as if her dad were sitting there next to her now.

She knew there wasn't a troll king. Just like she knew there weren't any ghosts in their basement or spaceships in their yard.

Tap-tap-tap.

But she also knew that *something* was definitely at her window. Claire swallowed down a whimper and slid out of bed, then crept toward the window. Holding her breath, she yanked up the shade before she could chicken out.

A pale face loomed in the darkness.

"Yah!" Claire fell backward, images of the underground kingdom flooding her mind—lanterns made of frozen dewdrops, twisty mazes with no exits, and trolls riding giant toads and keeping children as pets.

"Claire," the specter said. And she recognized the voice, and the face, even with its nose all smushed.

"M-Mike?" She got to her feet and switched on her bedside lamp, then opened her window, her heart still beating way too fast. "What are you doing here?"

"Ronnie said you're leaving in the morning. I wanted to say good-bye."

"Um, oh. Uh, okay." Claire took a step back. "Er, come in. But quietly, 'cause my dad..." Actually, she wasn't sure what her dad would do. A normal dad would not be okay with a boy sneaking into his twelve-year-old daughter's bedroom at night, but Claire knew her dad was anything but normal. Plus, it was *Mike*. "He'd probably want to hang out with us," she finished.

He slid through her window and dropped to the floor, then stood there awkwardly, his arms too straight at his sides. After a few seconds, he shoved his hands into his jeans pockets. "So."

"Yeah," Claire agreed. She was sure her face was flushed, and she could still feel her pulse jumping. And when had Mike gotten so tall? He was actually a few inches taller than her, now. And he was standing way, way too close. Should she take a step back? But then that might make things weird. Or, weirder. "Good-bye, I guess?"

"Before you leave," Mike said, not taking the hint, "I had to tell you that..." His voice trailed off, and he mumbled something so quietly that even standing literally inches from him, Claire couldn't understand.

"What was that?" she asked.

His face went beet red. "I said, Ronnie wasn't lying." He looked away, and now Claire could see how the red had crept out to the tips of his ears. "I *do* like you," he mumbled, but clearer this time.

Now Claire found *she* couldn't look at *him*, either. "Oh." She felt her face grow hotter and hoped it wasn't as red as his. "Um, thank you?"

Mike flinched as if she'd just smacked him in the face with one of Wrong Way's breadsticks, and Claire knew that whatever the right thing to say was, she'd just said the opposite.

"You don't like me back, do you?" he said.

"I . . . I *do* like you." She could stop there. She was leaving tomorrow, after all, and for the first time, that didn't seem like the worst thing ever. But as she looked up into Mike's hopeful, scrunched-up face, she knew she really couldn't.

He was her friend. He deserved honesty.

"But," she continued, and the hope in his eyes withered and died. Ugh. This was *horrible*. "I've just never really thought of you like, like that," she finished. She realized she was waving her hands around and tried shoving them into her pockets. Then she realized she was wearing her pajamas, the ones with owls and hearts all over them, and suddenly everything was So. Much. Worse.

Leaving tomorrow was sounding better and better by the second.

Mike nodded. "I understand." His voice was so sad she wanted to take it all back. Because really, she wasn't sure she didn't not like him, either. She didn't really know how she felt.

Instead, she just looked at the carpet, studying the worn spot by the corner of her bed. She hated how her dad never gave a straight answer, how he danced around everything he didn't want to talk about. But right now, she wished she knew how to change the subject as smoothly as he did. And then, suddenly, she *did* know. "What happened?" she blurted.

Mike blinked. "What?"

"This year. What happened to you? You got... quieter." *Sadder*, she almost said. But that wasn't quite right, either. She remembered how he'd hugged the walls at school like a ghost and barely even nodded at her when she passed, like he was hoping to disappear.

"Do you really want to know?" he asked.

"I do."

Mike let out a breath. "Nothing."

Claire frowned. "Mike—"

"It wasn't anything. Not really. Some of the other boys just said... a few things to me one day. They made me realize that..." He shrugged. "I just don't fit in there." He finally looked at her again. "I don't fit in anywhere."

Claire curled her hands into fists. "Who said something to you?" She wanted to hit them, every last one of them.

"No one important."

"Who, Mike?"

"Does it matter? They all think the same things. Even the ones who aren't saying it out loud." He sighed. "I wish I was going in that van with you."

"I wish you were, too."

He managed a smile. "Thank you." Then his face scrunched again, his eyes glistening. He turned away and ran the back of one hand across his face. "So embarrassing."

Claire's heart hurt. "It's not. It's normal."

"It's just, I'm really going to miss you, and—"

"Ha! Caught you," Ronnie hissed, sticking her head through the open window.

Mike jumped, then tripped over Claire's bed and ended up sprawled on the floor.

Ronnie laughed evilly.

"Shh," Claire hissed.

"Oh yeah, your dad might hear." She climbed inside and shut the window. "And then we'd never get rid of him." She leaned back against the wall. "I really am going to miss that guy."

"Um, excuse me?" Claire said.

"Oh, and you, too." Ronnie managed to hold her grin for another second before it slid off her face, and she rushed forward, hugging Claire, a classic awkward Ronnie hug, and

Claire didn't want to cry. She wasn't *going* to cry. But she couldn't help remembering a thousand sleepovers and camping trips and whispered secrets. Visits to waterparks and huddling in Ronnie's room, doing homework, or binge watching about ten hours of cartoons at a time until they both felt disgusted and swore they'd never watch television again, and ...

And she was going to miss her. She'd miss this life.

"You're going to have such a good time," Ronnie sobbed. "I'm so jealous."

That stopped Claire's tears immediately. Everyone always thought her life was more fun than it was, that her *dad* was more fun than *he* was. That everything was a Grand Adventure.

But it was a lie.

Claire pulled back. "It's not just some fun summer vacation," she said bitterly. "This is my life now."

"Just for now," Ronnie said.

"I told you, Dad sold the house."

"I still can't believe it." Ronnie shook her head. "Still. Eventually, you'll move ..."

"Move where?" Claire demanded. "Because wherever it is, it won't be back here."

Ronnie's shoulders slumped. "I know," she said quietly. She pulled a manila envelope out from her jacket pocket and handed it to Claire, her hands trembling. "I didn't have time to wrap it properly. Sorry."

Claire opened the envelope and pulled out a stack of what looked like postcards. They were all pre-addressed to Ronnie and stamped, but there were no pictures on the front.

"You're supposed to draw your own pictures," Ronnie explained. "I got you colored pencils, see?" Claire found them in the bottom of the envelope. "I thought you could illustrate the things you see. So it would be like I'm seeing them, too, but through your eyes."

Claire hesitated, the stack of pencils heavy in her hand. Then she dropped them back into the envelope and closed it. "Thank you. But you know I don't draw anymore."

"Not since you found the divorce papers," Ronnie pointed out.

Claire flinched.

"You found what?" Mike asked.

"Not your business, Mike." Ronnie held out her hand, palm toward him, her eyes never leaving Claire's face. "It's still okay to have fun sometimes, Claire. I promise. It's okay."

Claire had the strangest urge to fling the postcards in Ronnie's face. She *wasn't* afraid to have fun. "It has nothing to do with my mom. I just stopped because I realized I'm not that good."

"You're *really* good," Mike said. "You drew me that picture of a horse dancing on the moon, remember? I still have it."

"Yeah, but Mike, you're in love with her. Of course you think she's good."

Mike spluttered, and Claire felt her face going red all over again. "Ronnie!" she managed.

"What? I figured he was in here earlier professing his feelings. Right?" Neither of them would look at her, and she grinned wickedly. "Am I sorry I missed that!" She shook her head. "My point is that *I* also think you're good, Claire. And even if you were terrible, which you're *not*, you loved drawing. You shouldn't give it up just because it's not 'practical.'" She patted Claire on the shoulder. "And sorry, I know you hate air quotes."

Claire looked at her postcards, then stuffed them back in the envelope with the pencils. "Thanks," she said stiffly. She was so never using them.

"Just think about what I said, will you?"

Claire nodded.

"Well." Ronnie glanced around the empty room, her shoulders slumping. "I guess this is good-bye."

"I guess so," Claire said. She sniffed, then sniffed again.

"Keep in touch. Visit when you can. Tell me everything." Ronnie hugged her hard one more time, then hoisted herself out the window.

Mike hesitated. "She's never been good at good-byes," he said. "She cried all night, though."

"Ronnie did?" Claire couldn't picture it, but Mike never lied.

He gave her a quick hug that was somehow even more awkward than Ronnie's. "I'll miss you," he said into her hair, and then he was gone, too.

Claire stood at the open window for a long time.

CHAPTER 7

Claire's dad rolled his window down, then cranked the volume on the radio up until Claire couldn't think, her head filling with music and wind and the realization that this was happening, this was it. She was in a van.

She was living the hashtag vanlife.

Patrick had claimed the copilot seat for the first leg of their trip, which meant Claire was sitting on top of the cooler, the buckle of her dad's homemade seatbelt digging uncomfortably into her side. And did he even know how to make a seatbelt? Or how to fasten one properly? She tried not to imagine the seatbelt ripping free, sending her flying right through that giant windshield. Instead, she rested her forehead against the window and watched the edges of night curl away from the sky, leaving behind the soft blue glow of a perfect morning. It would be so much better if it were raining. Or thundering. Something to match the way she felt inside. Maybe a giant tornado would swoop down the road toward them, dark and swirling with menace.

"Chomps!" Patrick shrieked abruptly, so loud their dad swerved the van a little in surprise. "I forgot Chomps!"

Their dad actually turned down the volume on the radio. "You're sure?" he asked.

Patrick nodded, his forehead creased.

"Absolutely positively sure?"

Patrick nodded again.

Claire tensed. Chomps was Patrick's favorite toy, a dinosaur stuffed animal that their mom had bought for him before she left. The *only* toy she'd bought him before she left. But their dad had warned them when they headed out that anything left behind was left behind for good, so Claire waited for him to spin some tale about Chomps living a new life in the wilds of Michigan. Instead, he took the next exit and flipped around. "We can't exactly adventure without him, can we?" he said, his tone super reasonable, like *obviously* they needed a stuffed dinosaur along on this road trip.

"But we've already been driving for, like, an hour," Claire whined. She wasn't sure why she was arguing; she knew Patrick would feel terrible if they didn't go back for Chomps. And it wasn't like she was in a hurry to leave forever.

"We've got time," her dad said. "We've got nothing *but* time."

"Then why did we leave so early in the first place?"

"Because we're setting out on a *Grand Adventure*. Which means . . . what, Patrick?"

"It means we ride out with the sun," Patrick said promptly, giving a smile full of adoration, like his dad was some sort of superhero. And *that*, Claire realized, was why she'd been arguing. Part of her wanted Patrick to feel as miserable as she did, to see their dad the way *she* saw their dad. Immediately, guilt swirled around her, thicker and blacker than any tornado, and she kept quiet the rest of the drive to the house.

An hour later they were back on the road again, Chomps tucked securely under Patrick's arm. This time their dad left the radio off, the windows up, silence filling their van. "I promised you both a story for the road," he said.

"Can you tell us the one about Mom and King Mossofras?" Patrick asked, squeezing Chomps.

Somehow the silence got louder. Their dad hadn't told any stories about their mom in over a year, ever since Claire discovered the divorce papers.

"How about instead I tell you what happened when my grandfather made a deal with King Mossofras and—"

"Nope," Patrick said. "I want the one about Mom." He crossed his arms, getting that stubborn look he wore whenever Claire tried to get him to eat anything vegetable-related. One time, she'd gotten him to eat a spoonful of peas, and he sat there for over thirty-five minutes with them in his mouth. He had that look now, like he wasn't swallowing anything, especially his dad's excuses.

Their dad sighed. "It's an interesting story," he said resignedly. "Your, uh...your mother. And the king." He shifted his hands on the steering wheel. "I've told you how right after we met, I had to rescue her from His High—"

"His Mossiness," Patrick corrected.

"Sorry. Yes. From his hidden underground kingdom."

"By telling two truths and a lie, right?" Patrick leaned forward.

"By *guessing* two truths and a lie, actually. But the thing is...I guessed wrong."

"What?" Claire said, forgetting herself. This was a different spin on the old tale.

"The lie I guessed was really a truth. And one of the truths...was a lie." His knuckles whitened over the rim of the steering wheel. "Took me years to figure that out," he added quietly.

And Claire remembered his face that morning when she discovered those papers. He'd found her crouched over them and gently took them away, then folded them, again and again and again until his fingers shook with the effort of pressing the paper smaller, smaller. He hadn't said a word about them, though. Not then, and not in the year since.

"What were they?" Patrick asked. "The truths and the lie?"

Claire watched her dad's profile intently. Maybe today was the day he finally told them everything.

But he just shook his head. "I can't tell you that. Not today."

"Why not?" Patrick whined.

"Because once I do, I'll have only three days to live. So unless you want to be rid of your old man, you'll have to wait until you're older for the rest of that tale."

Patrick sighed and slumped against the door. "Is that why he came back for her, though? For Mom? Because you guessed wrong?"

"Something like that." Their dad glanced in his rearview mirror and changed lanes. "Anyone need to stop at the rest area? Two miles."

"No, Dad," Patrick said. "I want to hear the rest of the story. You can skip the truths and lie, so you don't die on us. Just tell us what happens after."

"That's very compassionate of you, Patrick. Very kind-hearted. I sure do feel loved and appreciated and adored."

He was looking for a way out, Claire realized. For once, her dad had talked himself into a corner, and he was looking for a story to save him. One that didn't involve their mom.

"What about Wrong Way Jacobus?" Claire blurted, hating herself for playing her dad's game. But even though Patrick was old enough to know their mom hadn't *really* been taken by trolls, or mimes, or lions, Claire didn't know what he actually believed... and she wasn't ready to find out. Better to let her be another story from their past, and keep her there. "You promised you'd tell us the rest of the story," she added.

"The rest of the story," their dad mused. "That's a tall order. Can't guarantee you'll get the *rest* of the story. For instance, I don't actually know what happened in those first long weeks when Wrong Way—he was still Edgar then, actually—when he left his village behind. I'm assuming he took a steamboat across the Atlantic Ocean, but for all I know, he caught a ride with a pod of whales."

"Whales." Patrick snorted. "Yeah, right." He still had his arms crossed tightly, his lips puckered in a sulky frown. One second away from a tantrum.

"Sounds like maybe you don't want to hear this story, eh, Patrick?"

Patrick shrugged.

"I mean, I don't *have* to tell it. It's an interesting story, definitely. Especially on account of how Wrong Way became a famous outlaw..."

Patrick's head tilted, like a dog hearing the rattle of a food bowl. "An outlaw?

"Wanted dead or alive, in fact. Preferably dead. But if you don't want to hear about all that, that's fine." Their dad sighed theatrically. "No skin off my old back."

Patrick held out for a few minutes, and then he uncrossed his arms. "Okay," he decided. "You can tell us that story."

"I can? Why, thank you. You have a generous soul, my son."

"I know."

Their dad grinned, his shoulders relaxing as he drove, getting into the story. Spinning its web. "As I was saying, one way or another, Edgar came to America. To New York, specifically."

"He *had* to go to New York, didn't he?" Claire said. "Through Ellis Island?"

Her dad shook his head. "Ellis Island wasn't open yet. This was back in the 1850s. No, Edgar came through a place called Castle Garden, on the southern tip of modern-day Manhattan."

Claire frowned. That sounded...factual. Was Edgar Jacobus a real person? Obviously, her dad's story about the bakery and the inedible bread was a lie, but...was there some truth to this tale?

Two truths and a lie.

Her dad's eyes met hers in the rearview mirror, and he winked.

"Ugh. Dad. Are you going to tell us the story, or aren't you?"

"Stick around, Claire-bear, and maybe I will."

"I can't exactly go anywhere," she grumbled. "So might as well get on with it."

"And with that enthusiastic, ringing endorsement, let me tell you how Edgar traveled from New York to California, earning his infamous nickname along the way."

CHAPTER 8

W hen Edgar arrived in America, he became immediately disoriented," their dad began, his voice taking on the rolling cadence of a long story. "He came here without a plan, with barely more than the clothes on his back."

"And the baguettes," Patrick added.

"That's right. The baguettes."

"Which he couldn't eat."

"No, Patrick, he could not eat them. Although he tried, as he crossed the big blue ocean, all he managed to do was gnaw the edges a little."

"Why did he come to America?" Claire asked. "If he didn't have a plan or anything."

"Because your great-*great*-*great*-grandfather—"

"You don't have to keep emphasizing it."

"—might not have had a plan," her dad continued smoothly, "but he did have a goal: to live a great big life. He pictured his narrow bed in his narrow room back in his uncle's bakery, and he realized he'd been given a narrow escape. What at first had seemed like a terrible, scary thing—to be forced from home—he vowed to turn into an exciting opportunity.

"But in the chaos of Castle Garden, Edgar felt lost. He remembered he was a young man from a small village. And he had nowhere to stay, and no place to go, and no friends to help him. He left Castle Garden, wandering the city, growing smaller and smaller inside until he was sure he would shrink into nothing. And then, just when he was feeling the most lost of all, he heard a scream . . ."

Something about that scream lodged straight inside Edgar's heart like a fishing hook, reeling him in. He raced toward it, so fast and so hard he churned the dirt road beneath his feet, turning it into a river of dust behind him.

Pinned against an imposing brick building, a girl struggled against two bushy-bearded men who were clearly trying to rob her. One of them had a hold of her suitcase, and the other had one of her wrists. She tugged at her bag and kicked at the men, still screaming at the top of her lungs. Several other people scurried nearby, but none of them stopped to help.

Edgar reached the group and swung one of his baguettes. *Crack!*

The first man went down.

Edgar swung the baguette at the second man...and missed.

The man let go of the girl and smiled, his gleaming pale eyes the color of the fog sucking at the ships in the harbor, and just as greedy. He advanced on Edgar, who swung his bread again.

Whap!

The man caught it in one giant hand...and crushed it in his fist.

Edgar stumbled back, horrified. That was his finest baguette, the one he used to chop wood and hammer posts.

"Bwah ha ha!" said the man. It wasn't a laugh, but a declaration, full of evil intent. It made Edgar long for his narrow bed in his quiet village, which suddenly seemed so impossibly far away. The man said something else, grinning to show off the whitest, straightest, most perfect teeth Edgar had ever seen, and Edgar wondered if he'd finally met someone with teeth sharp enough to eat his bread. Trembling, he pulled his remaining baguette out of his belt and held it in both hands like a club.

Wham! Smack! Bam!

The would-be robber staggered, putting his hands up to fend off the blows as the girl swung her bag at his head and kicked his shins. Edgar lunged and got in one good smack with his bread, and the robber turned and sprinted away, vanishing into the gloom.

Edgar turned to the girl. Just then the clouds parted and a ray of sunlight illuminated her lovely face. Her eyes were the fresh green of his uncle's fields back home, framed by waves of strawberry blond hair, and lips as full as—

"Dad," Claire said. "Seriously?"

Her dad blinked, coming out of his story. "I might have gotten a little carried away," he admitted.

"I liked the bit about the bread," Patrick said, munching on something. "Pretzel?" He offered the bag to Claire, who took a handful. "You can keep going with the story."

"But we get that the girl is beautiful. You don't need to go on and on about it." Claire bit into her pretzel.

"She *was* beautiful," her dad said. "The most beautiful girl Edgar had ever seen. Unfortunately, he spoke only a few words of English, and she spoke no French at all. He didn't even get her name before the rest of her family showed up, following the river of dust Edgar had created, and whisked her away. Despite the girl's protests, they left him there alone, with only his remaining baguette for company."

"What about the other robber?" Patrick asked. "The first one he knocked out?"

"Er, yes. He was there, too." Their dad cleared his throat. "Actually, he's rather important, because he's the one who told Edgar about all the gold in California."

"Gold?" Patrick's eyes widened.

"The Gold Rush," Claire said. "You'll learn about it in school. Assuming we ever go back." She shot a pointed look at her dad's back, but he didn't take the bait.

"Exactly so," he said instead. "The California Gold Rush. This other robber, who, as it happens, *did* speak French—"

"Convenient," Claire muttered.

"—told Edgar he'd never seen a handier man with a pair of breadsticks. 'Now that my brother has run off and left me behind, perhaps it's time for me to find a new brother,' he told Edgar. Your ancestor—note the lack of emphasis, Claire-bear, eh?"

"You pointing it out just adds *more* emphasis," Claire grumbled.

"Ah. My mistake. Well, this relative of yours wasn't sure he wanted to join forces with some kind of robber. But the robber ended up being very persuasive.

"His name was Johnny, and he told Edgar he'd heard there was gold just lying around in California, waiting to be picked up. 'If you help me get to California, I'll help you get your own share of the gold,' he promised, adding that he'd make amends to all the people he'd wronged, once he made his fortune."

"That sounds pretty weak," Claire said.

"Maybe so, but you've got to remember, Edgar had no friends in this place. He had no money. And he was down to his last baguette. Things were looking pretty grim for him, and the thought of a fortune in gold, just waiting to be picked up from the ground, well... you can imagine how that would have been hard to resist."

Claire thought of the bills that used to pile up on their counter back home, each slender envelope carrying enough weight to slump her dad's shoulders and add lines to his face. After a while, the bills stopped piling, but only because her dad just shoved them inside a drawer.

He cleared his throat. "Edgar decided to give Johnny a second chance. 'I'll go with you on two conditions,' he told him. 'First, you teach me English. And second, no more stealing from people.' Well, Johnny could agree to the first readily enough, but he told Edgar the second would have to wait; there was one last thing he needed to steal. And for that, he'd need Edgar's help."

"What did he want to steal?" Patrick asked, wide-eyed.

"A pair of horses. The fastest horses in all of New York, in fact. Dash and Flash."

Claire rolled her eyes, but her brother loved it. "Those are great names, Dad," he said.

"Did *our ancestor* help steal them?" Claire demanded.

"Nice emphasis, Claire-bear." She scowled, and her dad laughed. "No, Edgar refused. In fact, he only stole once in his entire life... but that's a story for later. This time around, he told Johnny they would need to get their horses another way, and instead of theft, he convinced the owner of Dash and Flash to give him the horses in exchange for several weeks of hard manual labor."

"Only several weeks?" Claire said doubtfully. "Aren't horses super expensive?"

"Well, Edgar was a persuasive, charming guy, much like yours truly." Her dad winked. "Besides, one week of his hard work equaled ten weeks from anyone else. But unfortunately for ole Edgar, those weeks cost them dearly; by the time he and Johnny made it to California, they were too late. The Gold Rush was over, and he had to make his fortune a different way."

"What way, Dad?" Patrick asked.

"What fortune?" Claire asked. That seemed the more important question.

"Good questions. Good, good questions. They'll have to wait, though, because we've arrived, my children. Feast your eyes on this."

Claire looked out the window, her eyes widening. Metal loops and swirls soared above the trees, against a backdrop of glittering water. "An...an amusement park? Really?" She could count the number of times her dad had taken them to an amusement park on one hand, and she'd still have a finger or two free. He claimed they were just too expensive. The last time she and Patrick had begged to go to one, he'd taken them hiking instead. "Nature is your amusement park," he'd said. "What can be better than this?"

He pulled into the giant parking lot, navigating the rows and parking near the tree line out back. There weren't too many other cars there yet, but Claire could see a line filling up the spaces behind them. Their dad texted someone, then stuffed his phone into his back pocket and fixed each of his kids with his most intense look. "You ready for our first adventure?"

"Ready," Patrick said solemnly. "Hashtag vanlife."

"Hashtag vanlife," their dad agreed, just as solemnly. He put his fist out and Patrick tapped it with his own.

Claire sighed.

"Say it," Patrick ordered, putting his fist out toward Claire. "You know you want to."

"I'm not saying it." She pushed his hand away from her, then looked again at the park, all glittering and beckoning and exciting. But then she noticed the way her dad's eyes gleamed, like his face was a jack-o'-lantern and someone had just lit the candle inside his head.

Excitement curdled in her stomach, turning to dread. Her dad always proposed his most outrageous, most ill-advised adventures when he had that look in his eyes.

CHAPTER 9

Claire followed her dad and brother to a small service gate tucked away on the edge of the parking lot. She could hear the noise of a lot of people having a great time: joyous shrieking and laughter and the mechanical *whizz* of rides. She took a deep breath. Cotton candy. She could *definitely* smell cotton candy.

Claire loved cotton candy.

But the entrance to the park was to the left, so why were they all the way over here?

The dread pooling in her stomach grew thicker and heavier until she thought she might be sick. "Dad," she started. "Why—"

"Scottie?" A man poked his head out from behind the nearest tree. He had a patch of facial hair under his lower lip, but the rest of his face was clean-shaven, his cheeks round like a baby's, and he wore an orange vest with a nametag clipped to the top.

"Julian!" Claire's dad gaped. "What happened to your beard? You were always so proud of that thing."

Julian ran a hand down his smooth chin. "Times change, my friend. But I still kept a little around as a souvenir." He tapped the patch under his lower lip and winked. "I just can't believe we both ended up back here, in the Midwest. And now Mac, too."

"What? No."

"Oh yes, back in beautiful Ohio. Wants nothing to do with me, for some reason."

Claire's dad grinned. "I can't imagine why." He turned to Claire and Patrick. "Kids, this here is Julian, my old college buddy."

"I thought you didn't go to college, Dad," Patrick said.

"No, I went...best year of my life." He grinned, and Julian roared with laughter.

Patrick wrinkled his forehead.

"He did two semesters," Claire whispered. "Then he met Mom. And then..." And then her mom got pregnant with *her*, and her parents both dropped out.

But Claire didn't really like to think about that.

Julian opened the small gate and glanced around. No other people were in sight. "Your kids know the drill, right?" he asked, dropping his voice.

"The drill?" Patrick asked.

Claire's mouth had gone dry. He couldn't possibly mean ... he didn't want them to sneak in, did he?

"*You*, my man, will have the easiest time of it." Julian rubbed Patrick's head. "No one thinks to question a young kid. Just pretend you're hurrying after your parents. And if you do get stopped, lie."

"Me? Lie?" Patrick smoothed his hair out.

"Yeah, lie, like a dog in the sun, eh?" Julian laughed again, loud and abrasive. "That's the other benefit to youth. No one expects you to lie to their face, so you can get away with just about anything."

"But, what do I say?"

"What's this? Your old man hasn't coached you up?"

"That's not really—" their dad began, but Julian was already talking over him.

"Tell them that your mom has your ticket, and she's just up ahead. And you're hurrying to find her. You can't act scared, though, or the attendant will feel like they need to escort you. Just act like you're impatient to catch up. Nine times out of ten, they'll just let you go."

"But what about the tenth time?"

"The tenth time?" Julian clapped him on the shoulder. "Smart kid."

Patrick staggered. "Um, thanks?"

"The tenth time, you run." Julian winked again.

Claire felt worse and worse the longer Julian talked, and when he looked at her, she shrank back a few inches. She couldn't lie. Could she? She couldn't sneak in. She looked up at her dad, her heart racing.

The gleam was gone from his eyes, his expression soft, careful. It reminded her of the look he wore when she was getting X-rays of her wrist, after she'd fallen out of his fort: guilty, like he was bracing himself for bad news.

"I'm not sneaking in," she said.

"Claire-bear—" he started, his tone all reasonable.

"No." She folded her arms. "Can't we just go in through the gate and pay for our tickets like normal people?"

He flinched, his face crumpling. *Distal radius fracture. Six weeks in a cast, and we'll want to X-ray again in three, just to make sure it's lining up properly.*

Claire rubbed her left wrist absently, but she wasn't backing down. She might live in a van now, but she still believed in rules. And the rules were, if you wanted to go to an amusement park, you had to buy a ticket. It didn't matter if they couldn't afford it. And she *knew* they couldn't afford it. After all, if a second round of X-rays wasn't in the budget, amusement park tickets definitely weren't.

But Claire told herself she was *not* going to think about how they never had enough money. And she was *not* going to think about how much fun those rides would be, or how her brother was looking at her like he might start crying, or about the taste of cotton candy melting on her tongue. Because rules were rules. And if she didn't follow them, then, then...

Claire sniffed. "I can't, okay, Dad? I'm sorry. I can't."

Her dad sighed, his shoulders slumping. "No, you can't," he agreed. He turned to Julian. "If we chose to go through legally, how much are the tickets?"

"Ooh, man, you never want to pay at-the-gate ticket prices. It's the worst deal in the park. Not counting the price of beer." Julian shuddered dramatically. "Twelve bucks for one lousy bottle, can you even believe it?"

"But ticket prices?" their dad prompted.

"Oh. Right. I think today they're going for forty-nine dollars per person, unless you're under four feet. Your boy might be on the line."

"Hmm."

Claire's shoulders felt like they were up at her ears. Forty-nine dollars per person? There was no way.

"You know, I think we're gonna pass for today," her dad said.

She froze.

"You sure? You can slip through here right now, won't cost a thing."

"Nah, that's alright. But thanks, Julian. I appreciate the offer, I really do."

Claire felt like she was standing on a line, and on one side there was nothing, nothing at all. For a second she thought of Wrong Way Jacobus, and how he must have felt when Johnny offered him a chance at the fortune of a lifetime, in exchange for one little theft. Horses . . . for gold. He'd turned it down, too. And then missed the Gold Rush.

Not that it mattered. It was just a stupid story. It didn't mean anything at all. Still, she couldn't help looking at that open gate.

"See you this evening?" her dad asked. "I was hoping we could talk about . . . you know."

Julian sucked on his lower lip, that patch of hair bristling. He nodded. "Brian mentioned you might want to chat. Not sure I have the best news for you."

"Julian. Come on, we've been friends for a long time."

"I know. I know, man. It's just . . . you see where *I'm* at, right?" Julian jerked a thumb at the park behind him. "And, no offense, but I got my degree. I mean, it's stupid, bunch of bureaucratic nonsense. But . . . supply and demand, my friend." He shrugged.

Someone called his name, and he glanced back over his shoulder. "I gotta run. But yeah, come on over, and we'll talk. Right? We'll talk. You have the address?"

"I have the address."

They exchanged a few shoulder slaps, while Claire mulled over the "you know," and the "we'll talk," and the "supply and demand." What was her dad up to?

"Alright, kiddos," he said. "Let's roll."

"Wait, Dad." Patrick tugged at his shirt. "Wait, we can just go in and—"

"Not today, Patrick. We'll come back here. Someday."

Someday. Which meant never. Patrick knew that as well as Claire did.

Patrick hung his head, staring down at his feet. Then he lifted those feet, first one, then the other, and trudged after his dad across the parking lot. Claire fell into step beside him. "Sorry, Patrick," she whispered.

He shrugged his thin shoulders and didn't look at her.

"It's just—" she began.

"You always ruin everything." He whirled toward her, the fury in his eyes stopping her mid-step. She expected him to start crying, but his eyes stayed hot and dry, and that was somehow so much worse. "Dad is *trying*. He's trying. And you . . . you just keep messing things up. Every time he has a fun idea, you just, you . . ." He threw up his hands. "You make it unfun."

Claire flinched. *Unfun.* In their family, there was no worse insult. Her dad had a motto. Okay, he had many mottos, but one of his favorites was *Be anything but boring.* "I don't mess up every—" she started.

"Whatever." Patrick spun on one sneakered foot and hurried away, leaving her behind.

"—thing," Claire whispered. It felt like all the air had left her lungs, her foot still raised as if she had forgotten how to walk in the middle of taking a step. Slowly, she lowered it. Ronnie had basically accused her of not having fun, too.

You always ruin everything.

She didn't. She was here, wasn't she? She was living in that stupid van, and she hadn't even made that big a fuss about it.

But you didn't help with the van. You didn't allow yourself to get caught up in the excitement. You won't even say hashtag vanlife.

Claire swallowed the lump in her throat. It tasted like the river of dust from her dad's story, and she watched as her brother caught up to him. Her dad tousled Patrick's hair and then hugged him briefly, before they both disappeared inside the van.

Neither of them looked back. Neither of them noticed her falling behind. Or maybe they did notice, and they just didn't care.

Unfun.

Claire squeezed her hands into fists, squeezed them until they went numb, but it didn't help.

CHAPTER 10

They spent the day hanging out on the shore of Lake Erie. Claire sat on the sand and pretended to read a book, but her eyes kept sliding over the words, the pages wavering like they'd been caught in a vicious heatwave.

Her dad and Patrick played in the water and looked for shells. Patrick had been mopey at first, but after his dad pointed out a piece of beach glass and told him about shipwrecks, her brother's mood had lightened.

Patrick never was able to stay upset for long. No wonder everyone liked him best.

Claire sighed and turned a page. Why did she have to be the way she was?

A wet blanket. She'd heard her dad use that expression before. Never to describe her, though. Her dad never said mean things about her, ever.

Even today.

Sitting there on the warm sand, watching the waves crash and tumble, Claire *felt* like a wet blanket. Heavy and uncomfortable and no fun at all.

She wasn't fun. She ruined everything. She was the worst. The worst. The worst.

"Claire-bear, you hungry?" Her dad sat next to her, water dripping off his nose and arms and trickling down his legs. "Your brother is making us all peanut butter and jelly sandwiches, with a healthy dose of sand. Good for the teeth." He bared his in a grin.

Claire shrugged.

"You okay?"

She shrugged again.

"There's no shame in wanting to follow the rules, if that's what this is about. There's no shame in that at all."

"*You* don't follow the rules," Claire accused.

He laughed. "True, but that's because I've learned that a lot of rules weren't really made for everyone. But the ones that matter? Those I follow."

"How do you know which ones matter?"

"If you think they're important, in here," he tapped his chest, "then they matter."

"Even if no one else thinks they matter?"

"*Especially* if no one else thinks they matter." He ruffled her hair, the same way he did Patrick's. Claire pushed his hand away, but her heart felt a little lighter. "My moral compass doesn't always point north, as I'm sure you've noticed. Your mother's didn't always, either." He looked away, like he was trying to see her across the lake. "How two such people managed to produce such a responsible kid..."

Claire's skin tightened, like the world was holding its breath. Her dad had brought up her mom, had said something *true* about her mom. Maybe they could finally, finally talk about her. A *real* conversation, without trolls or magic. She could tell him what she and Ronnie had found last summer. The photo, the new life, the condo in California... And he could tell her why her mom had left them. She opened her mouth—

"Do you think this place is haunted?" Patrick said, spraying sand all over the place as he rushed over, his hands full of beach glass. "You know, because of all the shipwrecks?"

"Absolutely," their dad said.

Claire closed her mouth again, the moment gone.

"Over two thousand ships, Claire!" Patrick dropped his finds on the sand next to her.

"More than any of the other Great Lakes," their dad said, "on account of how shallow it is." He ruffled Patrick's hair. "Now, what happened to those sandwiches?"

"Oops." Patrick laughed. "They've become sand-wiches!"

"Look at you, getting all clever. Just like your sister."

Claire waited for Patrick to make some snide remark, something about how he'd never be like her. *He* was fun, after all. But instead, her brother just smiled. "Want to swim with me, Claire?" he asked. "We can see who goes the farthest out. Loser has to make new sandwiches."

And for the first time all day, Claire relaxed. It was the same feeling she got when she tightened her hands into fists and then let her fingers uncurl on their own, like that tension she'd created was fading away.

After they were done swimming in Lake Erie, they rinsed off in the showers and then argued with their dad about visiting the Lake Erie Nature and Science Center. "Those are always boring, Dad," Patrick said firmly.

"Boring? Boring? I can't believe my ears. How could you possibly find a place like that boring? My child, sprung from my own seed."

"Eww, seriously, Dad?" Claire had refused to go to the museum after that, too, just on principle, and in the end, he drove them straight to Julian's house instead.

Julian's house was small, even smaller than their house. *Former* house, Claire corrected herself.

"Look at this driveway," her dad said as they pulled up. "Nice and wide and flat. Perfect for ole Van-Helsing."

"Can we please, *please* come up with a different name?" Claire asked as they climbed out of the van.

"Scottie!" Julian practically burst out his front door. "Welcome, welcome! You're just in time for dinner, and wait'll you see what I made."

"What, Chef Boyardee?" Claire's dad laughed.

"Just like the old days!" Julian clapped him on the back, laughing his loud, braying laugh.

"Wait, really?"

"Hey, you of all people can't complain. Remember that time you worked in the cafeteria?" Julian cackled. "Worst food I've ever eaten, and that's really saying something. I'm still surprised to this day they didn't fire you immediately."

"Oh, they wanted to. But it took them a week to finish the paperwork."

"He makes a mean crepe," Patrick spoke up.

"Is that so?" Julian looked their dad up and down. "Well in that case, I'm glad I went all out and added side dishes for you all."

Julian's side dishes turned out to be slightly stale garlic bread and a few wilted lettuce leaves pretending to be a salad. And a six-pack of beer, which he offered all around.

"Julian!" Claire's dad snapped. "Jeez! They're twelve and eight. They're not drinking beer."

"It was a joke. A joke." Julian waggled his eyebrows, but Claire noticed her dad was not laughing. Julian noticed, too. His eyebrows stopped their dancing. "What happened to you, man?" He glanced at Claire, then Patrick, eyes narrowing thoughtfully.

Claire's dad frowned. "Maybe it's time for that talk you promised me."

Julian sighed, his shoulders slumping. "Yeah, maybe."

"Do you have any games or anything for the kids?"

"Oh, sure, yeah. PlayStation in the back room. It's all set up. Have at it."

"Ooh," Patrick said, jiggling in his seat.

"Go on, then," their dad said.

"We haven't finished eating yet," Claire said. Not that she wanted to. But she kept thinking of that "you know" her dad had said at the park, and she wanted to hear more.

Her dad gave her a look she'd never seen on his face before. It reminded her of the looks Ronnie gave her when she was in danger of violating the friend code, only worse, sharp as a troll's fingers and twice as scary. Claire got up without another word and went with Patrick into the back room.

"Which game?" he asked.

"Whichever. Your choice." Claire strained her ears, trying to overhear the conversation in the other room. It was very quiet, but she caught a few words.

Julian's voice saying something, something, "tight around here..." something else..."better luck in Elmsborough...Mac might..."

Better luck? Claire tilted her head.

"...not sure about seeing Mac again," her dad said.

So frustrating! Why didn't her dad talk louder?

"Oh, that was a long time ago. Water under the bridge!" Julian guffawed. He, at least, was plenty loud.

"Which controller?" Patrick asked.

"Hmm?" Claire blinked, missing the next thing Julian said. Sounded like a question. "Oh, whichever," she told Patrick.

She thought she heard her dad say something about "the kids," and everything inside her went still.

Video game music blasted through the room. Patrick tossed a controller at Claire and settled down, his small face scrunched into a very serious expression.

"Can we turn down the music?" Claire asked.

"Nope," Patrick said. "It helps me concentrate. Plus, you owe me."

Claire thought of the glimmering rides she'd forced him to pass up and didn't argue. But she didn't let Patrick win, either.

He still beat her twice anyhow.

CHAPTER 11

"If you need to use the bathroom, use it now or forever
hold your pee."

"Ha ha, Dad," Claire said. "You're so funny. So funny."

"I've often thought so." He grinned as he got his mattress situated, turning it from a couch into a bed, then
pulling the pillows and blankets out from the rolling
shelf hidden beneath. "Give me a hand with these sheets,
and then we'll get your hammocks set up."

They were still in the driveway next to Julian's house;
he'd chatted with Claire's dad for only about an hour before
they called it a night. Claire got the feeling her dad was
ready to be away from his old friend. Would she feel the
same way about Ronnie, the next time she saw her? Like
they'd grown into separate people who didn't actually like
each other all that much?

She thought of those postcards, stuffed into the bottom of her backpack. Ronnie wanted her to illustrate them with the things she saw on this trip. *So it would be like I'm seeing them, too, but through your eyes.* Would that help her and Ronnie stay friends?

"It's not so bad here, is it?" her dad asked.

Claire hesitated. She hated to admit it, but it was actually kind of nice in the van right now. They had both of the back doors open, as well as the side door, and a gentle summer breeze swept through their van. Outside, stars sprinkled across the darkening sky while lightning bugs buzzed and glowed in the yard across from them. "It's . . . survivable," she decided. "Although I'm still not so sure about these hammocks."

"They're comfortable," Patrick said. "I already tested them."

"When?" Claire asked.

"I slept in here last night." He bounced on the balls of his feet.

"You did?" Their dad raised his eyebrows, surprised. "By yourself?"

"Don't worry, Dad. I checked for snipes first. None of them saw me."

Claire pictured her little brother, so excited about this newest Grand Adventure that he'd crept out into the van by himself. Her brother, who was scared of trolls, sleeping alone in his little hammock. Guilt washed over her, followed by an immense wave of sadness. She remembered being like Patrick, eager to join in on her dad's newest fantasy. She wished she were still like that.

No, she didn't. You couldn't live forever in a fantasy, in a *lie*. Claire pulled the edge of the sheet so hard, it almost slipped out of her dad's grasp.

"Watch it there, Claire-bear." He tightened his grip, laying the sheet down carefully. "And see? Hammocks are officially Patrick-approved, the very highest certificate of approval there is."

"Patrick approves almost everything," Claire grumbled.

"Hmm. Maybe Claire-approved is the ultimate goal, then."

"Claire never approves anything," Patrick said.

"Then it seems we're at an impasse—ah, hey, Julian. I thought you'd turned in for the night."

Julian poked his head around the side of the van. "Just wanted to get a look at the old beast."

"Here she is, in all her glory." Their dad extended his arms proudly.

"Very cool." Julian looked up and down the small space. "Not a lot of room, though."

"What are you talking about? It's downright spacious in here. Right, kids?"

"Right, Dad," Patrick said. Claire didn't say anything.

"Well, Scottie, my offer to use the guest room still stands, if you and the kiddos would like."

"No can do. We're living the hashtag vanlife right now."

"Dad, seriously," Claire muttered.

"Hashtag hashtag," Patrick whispered next to her.

"Stop it."

"If we ended up sleeping inside a house on this, our maiden night, well ... that would make us what, Patrick?"

"Vanlife tourists." Patrick wrinkled his nose.

Their dad laughed. "Exactly. And nobody likes a tourist."

"We're traveling everywhere in a van," Claire said. "Doesn't that make us, like, continual tourists?"

"Not at all. As long as we're sleeping in our van, we're golden."

Claire couldn't see the logic in that, but then, she couldn't see the logic in a lot of things her dad said. Like the whole troll thing, which had been going on for as long as she could remember. Why? Why trolls? Or this new story, this "Wrong Way" story. What was the point?

"Something wrong with your neck?" he asked. "You keep shaking your head."

"Yeah, I have this strange pain in it," Claire grumbled. "He's about five foot ten and extremely irritating."

He laughed. "Aww, Claire-bear, we're going to have so much fun on this trip! Here, take the end of this hammock, would you?"

"Alrighty then." Julian rubbed his hands together. "See you in the morning for breakfast?"

Claire glanced at her dad. He was making his thinking face, like he was trying to come up with an excuse not to stick around. Was there a Chef Boyardee breakfast equivalent? "Er," he said. "Well, we'd hate to impose any further—"

"Not at all! Besides, I figured you'd be the one making it!" Julian laughed again, the sound echoing through the van. Claire had never met anyone who laughed as loud or as often. "I have it on good authority that you make one heck of a mean crepe."

"He does," Claire said immediately. He might be a weirdo with a troll obsession, but Claire could admit her dad *did* make a mean crepe.

"Too bad he only makes them on Sundays," Patrick added.

Julian gave him a strange look, then shrugged. "See you bright and early." He saluted all of them, then left.

Patrick shook his head. "He has no idea."

"He really doesn't," their dad agreed. "Poor fool. You can't make crepes if it's not Sunday. Not unless you want to be cursed."

"I think you're just lazy," Claire said, helping her dad slide the first hammock into place. "You just don't like making pancakes more than once a week."

"How dare you. Do I need to remind you of what happened to your aunt Jan?"

"She made pancakes on a Saturday?" Claire guessed.

"Oh, it's much worse than that." He helped her put up the second hammock. "It was a Tuesday. And everyone knows Tuesdays are . . . what, Patrick?"

"Tuesdays are not to be trifled with," Patrick recited immediately.

It was another of their dad's mottos: All the worst things that can happen to a person happen on a Tuesday. His theory was that you'd prepare for a Monday, and then Tuesday would sneak right in and sucker punch you in the gut.

Their mother had left on a Tuesday.

Claire finished setting up her bed, then tugged Ronnie's postcards from her backpack. She ran her finger over the smooth blank surface of one of them and imagined the feeling of a pencil scraping across it, picturing what she'd draw, if she still drew. Maybe the shores of Lake Erie, Patrick's pile of beach glass, the ghostly outline of an old ship . . .

"What's that?" Patrick asked.

"Nothing." Claire shoved the stack of blank postcards back into her backpack, thrusting the ideas away with it. She caught Patrick staring. "And you'd better not go poking around my stuff."

"You don't have a door to shut on me anymore." He stuck his tongue out.

"Dad!"

"Claire!"

Claire sighed. Her dad would be no help, as usual. "Whatever. I'm going to bed." She'd claimed the hammock closest to the back doors, which meant she had to clamber over Patrick's hammock first and then leapfrog across to her own. As she settled into it, the fabric hugged her body, and with her blankets pillowed at her feet, it wasn't actually that bad. Almost comfortable, even.

She closed her eyes and listened to her dad shutting the doors and setting the fan in the ceiling to bring in fresh air, and she imagined that blank postcard, still trying to decide if she should fill it in. Outside, the insects chirped and the breeze tapped chilly fingers against the side of their van, gently rocking her to sleep.

CHAPTER 12

Claire woke abruptly to the sounds of something large shuffling around underneath her bed. Her heart squeezed, her body frozen as the darkness pressed in on all sides. And where was she? This wasn't her room. It wasn't her bed!

And then she remembered: Van. Driveway. Hammock. Hashtag vanlife. And that shuffling noise was just her dad, doing some kind of reorganizing below her, the curtains still drawn tight. "What time is it?" she croaked.

"Four thirty," her dad whispered.

"In the *morning?*"

"Shh," he hissed.

"What's going on?" Patrick asked sleepily, and Claire felt him sit up in the hammock next to hers.

"We're going into stealth mode," their dad said. "Are you both in?"

"Absolutely," Patrick said immediately.

"What's stealth mode?" Claire asked suspiciously.

"Doesn't matter," Patrick said. "It sounds awesome. Like we're a spaceship."

"Exactly so," their dad said. "We're going to keep the hammocks up, keep the curtains drawn, and sneak out of this driveway like a black dog in the night. Secret. Silent. *Unseen*."

"So . . . basically you really don't want to make breakfast," Claire said.

"You say tomato. I say *stealth mode*."

"Dad, that doesn't even make sense."

"I call copilot!" Patrick was already hopping out of his hammock, and Claire reluctantly climbed down from her hammock, too, and took her seat on the cooler. This was so silly.

"Ready, crew?" their dad whispered.

"Ready, captain," Patrick said.

"Claire-bear?"

So, so silly. Claire sighed loudly.

"I can't fly into potentially dangerous enemy territory until I know I have the support of my full crew," her dad said.

"Ready," Claire muttered. "But I'm *not* calling you captain. Especially not after you woke me up at four in the morning."

"What if I promise to steer us somewhere with chocolate chip pancakes?"

Claire loved chocolate chip pancakes, and normally her dad didn't let her get them, because he believed *break-fast* and *dessert* should be two separate things. "Fine," she decided.

"Fine ... what?"

"I'm ready, *captain*."

He chuckled as he turned on the van, the diesel engine rumbling to life. And for a second, Claire could almost imagine they *were* in a spaceship soaring through the night, so silent the people below wouldn't notice them. Just another star in the sky, heading for parts unknown.

"So, Dad," Claire said, setting her fork down on her now-empty plate and staring at him across the table. They were in one of those twenty-four-hour, breakfast-served-all-day diners, the kind with plastic benches that clung to your skin and tables that always felt sticky.

"So, daughter." He grinned and waggled his eyebrows.

Claire resisted the urge to roll her eyes, and instead asked, "Were you planning on telling us where we're going?"

"Wherever we want. That's the beauty of hashtag vanlife."

"Okay. I get that you think that. But where are we *going*?" she repeated.

"Hmm ... I guess we should decide on our next destination."

"East!" Patrick howled. "East!"

"Stop it, Patrick," Claire said. "You're being disruptive."

"We're the only customers," he pointed out.

"Fine," Claire conceded. "But, a direction is not a plan."

"Yes, it is."

She frowned. "It's not a good enough plan."

"Let's see Castle Garden!" Patrick clapped his hands excitedly. "We can see where Wrong Way first came here, and then trace his route."

"That's an idea," their dad said slowly. "We can certainly go there, if that's what you both want... but you might be disappointed in Castle Garden."

"Is it still open?" Claire asked.

"Well, technically... yes. But I think it's just a place where vendors sell overpriced hot dogs and T-shirts. And there are bathrooms."

Claire wanted to see it, but if the hot dogs and T-shirts were overpriced, everything else would be, too. She glanced down at her empty plate, then over at the even emptier spot on the table in front of her dad where there was no plate, just coffee. The glimmer of a realization oozed inside her, stickier than any diner table. Next to her Patrick chanted, "Castle—Garden—Castle—Garden—" Oblivious. Happy.

The chocolate chip pancakes in Claire's stomach lurched and twisted, congealing into a lump of guilt. "I don't know, Patrick," she said, forcing the words out. "Sounds like an awfully long way to go for a bathroom." She met her dad's gaze just in time to see him flinch. It made her think of that day they couldn't afford her next round of X-rays, how he hadn't said a word, but afterward had called up their old neighbor Meredith. When he finally agreed to work under the table in Meredith's auto shop, he'd made that same pained expression.

Her brother stopped chanting, his forehead creasing. "Hmm," he said, considering.

"Maybe..." Their dad cleared his throat. "Maybe it's just not grand enough for our Grand Adventure. After all, if Patrick wants to go east—"

"East!" Patrick bellowed. The waiter in the corner turned and glared at them. "East," he repeated, a little softer.

"Then by all means, we must go east." Their dad beamed, looking again like his normal, eager, irritating self. "So maybe we should go all the way to the easternmost state. Which is ... Patrick?"

"Maine!"

"Exactly so, my boy, my clever protégé. We shall head to Maine."

"What's Maine like?" Patrick asked.

"Cold," Claire said.

"It's practically July," her dad said. "I doubt it'll be cold right now. And we can take Route 20 there. And you know what's special about that road?"

"I'm sure you'll tell us," Claire muttered.

"It stretches all the way from the Pacific Northwest to New England! To Boston, Massachusetts, if I'm not mistaken, making it the longest road in the US." He got up, Claire and Patrick following him as he paid their bill at the cash register, then headed out to the parking lot.

The sun was just brushing past the horizon, the day brightening all blue and cheerful. A couple of cars had pulled into the parking lot. Claire could feel the people in the car next to them watching as she pulled open the side door of the van.

A sock tumbled out, then a book and an empty water bottle.

Red-faced, Claire hurriedly picked them up and shoved them inside. After going into "stealth mode," they hadn't really organized, and already the inside of the van looked a little like Patrick's bedroom. It made her irritable, everything all messy like that. "Don't most people head west?" Claire demanded as she slammed the side door shut, then started folding blankets and shuffling clothing away. "Isn't that, like, a thing?"

"Yeah, but we're related to Wrong Way Jacobus," Patrick said. "So we have to go the wrong way!" He laughed.

"Clever boy," their dad said. "Claire, we can organize later. Let's hit the road."

"Copilot!" Claire yelled, realizing her brother had forgotten to call it.

"Aww, not fair," Patrick whined.

"Suck it up, buttercup." Their dad turned on the engine. "We've got a lot of miles to cover on the way to Maine, so let's roll."

"Fine," Patrick grumbled, flopping onto the cooler seat. "But I won't forget this betrayal."

Claire decided she was too mature to stick her tongue out at her brother, so instead she made a point of leaning back in the front seat, kicking off her shoes, and sighing contentedly.

"Don't get too comfortable there, *copilot*," her dad said. "I might need you to help navigate."

"What? You didn't make Patrick work when he was up here," Claire grumbled.

"Patrick didn't make a big production of it and then settle in like a smug bug."

"Smug bug!" Patrick laughed.

Claire shot her dad a look.

"No?" He raised his eyebrows, grinning. "I thought it was pretty good, personally."

"Yeah, you would," she muttered. "Where's the stupid map?"

"There's no such thing as a *stupid* map. But the *road atlas* is wedged under my seat. I don't need directions right now, so you can rest easy. Just be ready; I might call on you at any moment."

"Can't wait," Claire sighed, adding, half under her breath, "stupid map." Her dad always insisted on lugging that atlas with them on road trips, forcing Claire to squint at the squiggly roads and figure out which direction to go if they got lost, instead of using GPS like a normal human. She'd been hoping that might change on this trip with the addition of her dad's fancy new smartphone, but clearly it wasn't going to.

"You know," her dad said slowly as he pulled out of the parking lot, "we'll be driving right through Cleveland."

"And ... that's a good thing?" Claire asked.

"Oh, it's a very good thing. Because you know what's in Cleveland?"

"The Rock and Roll Hall of Fame!" Patrick said proudly.

Their dad was actually speechless for a whole twenty seconds. Claire counted silently. "Well. That was ... impressive," he managed. "I didn't realize you knew that. And yes, exactly so. But perhaps even more impressive is that Cleveland has a truly amazing natural history museum!"

"Dad," Patrick and Claire whined.

"I'm pretty sure it has a whole dinosaur exhibit."

"Really?" Patrick tilted his head, thoughtful, Chomps cradled on his lap.

"Don't fall for it, Patrick," Claire warned. "It'll still be boring, and we'll be there forever while dad talks to *everyone*. Trust me. I've seen it. I've done it. I don't need a reminder, dinosaurs or no."

"They probably have a space exhibit, too," her dad said. "Maybe a whole planetarium."

A planetarium. Back when Claire was six and into her space phase, she'd been obsessed with the idea of going to a planetarium. It was why her dad had bought those glow-in-the-dark stars for her ceiling, so she could have a planetarium in her room every night. Her ceiling, which she'd never see again. "I don't care about that stuff anymore," she said.

"Really?" Her dad frowned.

Claire shrugged, unwilling to take it back.

After a moment, he sighed. "Fine then. Tell you kids what: I'll just drive us on east, and if we feel like stopping at a museum or two? Well, so be it."

"We're not going to feel like it," Claire said.

"And if our van just happens to stop at a museum," he continued, "well, who can argue with Van-Helsing?"

CHAPTER 13

Claire leaned against the window and closed her eyes, the glass warm against her cheek. She dozed until her dad began wailing the lyrics to his new favorite song about some fool who got himself killed for love. It made her think of Edgar, and the beautiful girl he saw in New York.

"Was that girl Evangeline Rose?" she asked, sitting up.

Her dad stopped singing. "What's up, pup?"

Claire shook her head. "No. Just, no."

He grinned. "I thought I'd test it out. I'll keep trying."

"Do you have to?" Claire sighed and rubbed her left temple. "The girl in the story. The one who you spent, like, an hour describing yesterday—"

"Barely ten seconds, if that."

"Whatever. Is that our great-great-great-grandmother?"

Her dad's grin widened. "You're interested in this story, aren't you, Claire-bear?"

Claire shrugged.

"I haven't seen you interested in one of my sagas since—" He stopped abruptly, and Claire knew he was thinking of that moment when he'd found her crouched over the divorce papers.

He glanced in the rearview mirror at Patrick, who was asleep on the cooler seat. Then he shifted his gaze to Claire. Her heart thumped and rumbled like the diesel engine's vibrations beneath her feet as she waited for him to finally say something about her mom. Something true.

"Yes," he said, and Claire caught her breath, before he continued, "the woman in the story is Evangeline Rose. But you'll have to wait until your brother's awake before I tell the rest."

Claire sagged against her seatbelt. What had she been thinking? Of *course* her dad wouldn't tell her anything important. She scowled. "You know, Dad, sometimes it would be nice if you'd tell a *true* story for once."

"This *is* a true story," he said, offended. "More or less."

"I meant a true story about you. About now. *This.*" Claire waved her hands to take in the van. "I mean, I don't know where we're going, or what we're doing, or even where this van came from."

"We're going to Maine."

"What about *after* Maine?"

"I ... haven't figured that out yet. But that's the beauty of vanning, Claire-bear. We don't have to *have* a set destination, or plan. We can go where the road takes us, and just ... see what happens."

"Whatever." Claire closed her eyes and leaned her face against the window again. Her dad was never going to tell her the truth. It was like he wasn't capable of talking about anything important. Anything *real*.

If he noticed she was upset, he didn't act like it. Nope, he just went right back to singing, tapping his fingers against the steering wheel, having his stupid Grand Adventure.

Claire blinked. It took her a second to realize they had stopped driving. She sat up, her cheek all hot and sweaty from where it had been mashed against the window for too long. "Where are we?"

"Still in Ohio." Her dad unbuckled his seatbelt and opened his door. "Just making a brief stop, visiting another old friend."

"Like Julian?"

He grimaced. "Hopefully not. But possibly ... yes. Which is why I want the two of you to stay put, okay? I'll just be a few minutes." He closed the door. Claire craned her neck, watching her dad walk down the street and knock at the door of a brick house. A woman answered. A pretty woman with long dark hair, crimped and flowing down her back like a fairy princess. She stepped back, and Claire's dad followed her, vanishing inside the house.

"Did you see that?" Claire turned around.

Patrick sat up and rubbed the sleep from his eyes. "See what?" he yawned.

"Dad just met some woman."

"So?"

"So . . . she was pretty. And he's in her house. And he didn't want us to meet her." Claire felt too hot, her shirt sticking to her back. "Clearly something is going on."

"Like what?" Patrick asked.

Claire brushed her sweaty bangs back from her face. She wasn't sure what to say; her dad hadn't dated anyone since her mom left. *That you know of . . .* Still. It was probably nothing. Unless it wasn't. "Should we go spy?"

Patrick shook his head.

"Why not?"

"If even King Mossofras couldn't sneak up on him, we really don't have a chance."

"Stop being ridiculous. You know dad just made him up, right?" she snapped, before she could stop herself.

Patrick looked away, not answering.

Claire immediately felt terrible, like she'd just kicked a puppy. "Look," she sighed, "it's really hot in here. And I don't know how to work Dad's fan. Maybe we should just … step outside for a minute? To cool off?"

Patrick tilted his head. "And if we happen to see that woman…"

"That's not spying," Claire finished. "It's just luck."

Her brother grinned. "Are *you* breaking a *rule*?"

"No!" Claire said immediately. She chewed her lip, then added, "Maybe just a little."

Patrick put his fist out, and after a few seconds' hesitation, Claire bumped it with her own.

They slipped out of the van, and headed down the street. The woman's brick house looked totally ordinary. Claire opened her mailbox.

"Claire!" Patrick hissed.

"Just checking, okay?" There were only two envelopes and a *Dog Fancy* magazine, all addressed to a Mackenzie Sullivan. This must be the "Mac" Julian had mentioned.

Claire shut the mailbox, thinking again of the postcards Ronnie had given her. Ronnie would be so interested in this secret meeting between her dad and a mysterious woman. Claire knew her friend would want to hear all about it, and stealth mode, and heading east. Maybe she *would* send her a postcard after all. She didn't have to draw on it, but Ronnie needed to know about these new developments.

"Who do you think she is?" Patrick asked, cupping his fingers around his eyes like a pair of binoculars.

"Maybe an old girlfriend?"

Patrick stiffened. He dropped his hands and turned to face her. "That's not funny."

"It wasn't supposed to be." Claire pictured her dad the way someone else might see him, with his plaid shirts and ridiculous hats, and his stubble from not shaving in two days. Not that he ever managed to grow more than a few patches of facial hair. She tried to imagine him dating someone, and the picture of her mother swam through her memory, her mother with her short hair and laughing face, that stranger in the photo Ronnie had shown her. Claire wished she'd never seen it; it made it impossible to remember what her mother used to look like.

"Why would he be visiting an old girlfriend?" Patrick asked.

"Maybe he's . . . I don't know." Claire shut the mailbox.

"Mom's going to come back, you know," Patrick said.

All the air left Claire's lungs. "What?" she gasped.

"That's really why we're in a van. We're going to rescue Mom. Just like Wrong Way Jacobus rescued that lady in New York."

Claire took a deep, slow breath, everything inside aching. For a second, she'd thought Patrick knew something. "Patrick . . ."

"Don't give me that look. I'm not being a baby, okay?"

"But, rescue Mom from *what*?" Claire crossed her arms. "You know she's not actually trapped by the troll king, or stuck in a lion's den, or . . . or whatever silly story Dad comes up with next. They're just stories. You *know* it. We both know it. She's just gone, okay?"

"Whatever, Claire. You'll see." He looked so certain, with his large blue eyes all screwed up, his lips pressed together. It was the face he wore when he was deadly serious about something, usually a troll hunt or a new video game.

Claire fought down a burst of anger. Her brother was old enough to know better. It was their dad's fault, always telling stories. For a second she almost told Patrick about the divorce papers she'd found, but she stopped herself. Her dad should be the one to tell him about those. Instead, she squeezed her hands into fists, then said, as calmly as she could, "Mom's been gone almost eight years. Don't you think Dad would have gone after her years ago if he thought he could bring her back?"

Patrick looked stubbornly away, but his lower lip quivered, and just like that, Claire's anger wavered too, growing heavy and sad, like a balloon filling slowly with sand. She shook out her fingers. "I guess we'll see," she sighed.

"Yeah. We will."

It was too hot here, even outside the van, the air humid and sticky. "Let's take a walk, okay? Dad might be a while."

Patrick looked like he wanted to keep arguing, but then his face brightened. "I think there's a park down there! Want to race to it?"

"Sure—" Claire started. Before the word had left her mouth, Patrick took off. "Hey, not fair!" And by the time she caught up to him, she'd almost, *almost* forgotten about the woman with the pretty hair, and Patrick's theory, and her mother.

CHAPTER 14

Claire tilted her head. "Do you hear yelling?"

"Nah, that's just the soccer players over there." Patrick jerked his chin over to the nearby field where a group of kids kicked a ball around.

"No, it's not them." She knew it wasn't because one of the players was an extremely cute boy, tall with thick, curly black hair. He'd smiled at her when she and Patrick first arrived at the park, and she'd been sneaking glances at him ever since.

More yelling.

Claire frowned. "It sounds like—"

"Dad."

"Yeah, kinda."

"No, it *is* Dad. Look." Patrick pointed. Their dad was jogging toward them, and he *never* jogged. For a man who had so much energy, he'd always hated exercise for the sake of exercise. "What's the point?" he'd say. "I could burn just as many calories fixing the ole car, and at least then I'd have accomplished something." Unless it was hiking. He'd hike all day if you let him.

"He looks mad," Patrick whispered.

"Definitely," Claire whispered back.

Patrick inched closer until his shoulder brushed her side. It made her feel strangely powerful, like she was Wrong Way Jacobus holding her bread-weapon, ready to defend her innocent little brother.

"I'm totally blaming you," he added, and suddenly he didn't seem so innocent anymore.

"I *told* you to wait in the van," their dad snapped as he got within range. Both Claire and Patrick flinched back. "Do you have any idea how I felt when I got back there and you were both gone?" He crossed his arms, nostrils flaring. "Now, I'm pretty lenient, but that is *not* acceptable. Not when we're on the road. I need to know you'll stay where I leave you." He gave them both one last searing look. "Let's go." He turned and strode back across the park. For someone so concerned with their whereabouts, he didn't bother to look back and see that they were following him.

They followed him anyhow. Where else would they go?

"I thought you were going to blame me," Claire whispered.

"I still might," Patrick said. "But I think right now it would just make him angrier."

When they got back to the van, their dad unlocked the doors and threw them open, every movement jerky, his face locked in a scowl.

"Careful or your face might freeze that way," Claire said.

His scowl grew more fearsome.

Patrick elbowed her in the side and shook his head. Then he turned to their dad. "Why did you want us to stay in the van?"

"Because I *wanted* this to be a short stop. I didn't *want* to have to go traipsing all over this town."

"Who was that lady?" Patrick mirrored his dad's posture, crossing his skinny arms and standing with his legs hip-distance apart.

"I told you, she's an old friend."

"Claire thinks she's an old *girlfriend*, and that's why you didn't want us to meet her."

Claire was both annoyed that her brother had dragged her into this and impressed by his manipulative skills; by asking these questions, he'd put their dad on the defensive. Now their dad either had to give them information, which he hated to do, or backtrack.

She didn't give her brother enough credit.

"Why would you think that?" their dad finally asked.

Patrick shot Claire a look. Now *she* was in the hot seat. "Because . . . she has princess hair?" It sounded so dumb, the moment she said it, but it was too late. "And you totally shut us out," she added.

"She's not an old girlfriend," he sighed.

"Told you," Patrick whispered smugly.

Claire rolled her eyes. "Then who is she?"

"She's . . ." He put a hand to the back of his neck, rubbing the muscles there like he used to do after a long day of work. "She's your mom's old college roommate."

"Oh," Claire and Patrick said.

"Yeah. Oh."

"Why did you want to see her?" Claire asked.

"Oh, just a trip down memory lane. You know Julian used to go out with her?"

"What? Really?" Claire couldn't picture that pretty lady with all the hair dating Julian and his soul patch.

"It's how I met your mother, actually."

Was this . . . something true? Claire studied her dad's face. He didn't look angry anymore, or eager the way usually did when spinning a tale. He didn't look like anything at all, his face completely blank. It made her nervous, like she was watching her father get erased from the inside out.

And then she realized he'd told them something true . . . to distract them from something else. The real reason he'd wanted to visit this woman, Mackenzie.

"Would you look at that?" he said abruptly, shielding his eyes against the sunlight and staring at something behind them.

Claire turned. The first thing she noticed was the entire pack of dogs headed their way. Then she realized they were all leashed to two people, a grumpy-looking man with too-long hair and a surprisingly beautiful woman, both wearing hip packs and walking like this was something they did every day.

"Do you think they'll let us pet their dogs?" Patrick rubbed his hands together like he might leap out and snatch one.

"You could ask," their dad suggested.

"I wouldn't," Claire warned. "That man looks like he wants to murder you and turn you into dog food."

The man in question scowled at her.

"I think he heard you," Patrick whispered.

The woman looked friendlier, at least. She smiled as they got closer. "Nice van! Are you all camping?" she asked.

"We're hashtag vanlifing," Patrick said.

"Well, aren't you cute." She slowed down, peering through the open doors.

"What is this, a walk or what?" her companion demanded.

"Just a moment," the woman said. "I'm interested in this van."

"Be interested on your own time, then. We're on dog time here."

The woman rolled her eyes. "I'll add an extra minute to the end of their walk, okay, Wes?"

"Good business, dog walking?" Claire's dad asked, eyeing all the dogs. There were eight . . . no, nine. Actually ten, Claire realized; Wes, the grumpy dog walker, had a small pup half-hidden behind the larger dogs in his pack. It looked just like a little wolf.

"Don't even think about it, buddy," Wes said. "There are more than enough dog walkers in this town."

The woman laughed nervously. "Yes. Well. We'd better get going." She clucked at her pack, and all of them moved forward except a yellow Lab, who moved sideways instead, leaning against Patrick.

"Aww." Patrick pet her on the head.

"Sweetpea!" Wes barked, and the lab reluctantly moved back into formation. "No petting the dogs. They're working. As are we." He shot one last glare around at everyone, then flicked the leashes like the reins of a horse and set out.

"Good luck with your vanlife!" the woman called as she hurried after him. "Don't you think we could use a van like that?" she said to Wes as she caught up. "We could fit all the dogs in at one time and..." Her voice faded.

"Dad?" Claire said.

Her dad blinked. "Sorry. Distracted."

"She *was* a very pretty lady," Patrick said. "Even if the man looked like he might be part troll."

Their dad laughed. "You might very well be right about that, Patrick. No human can scowl quite so ferociously. Now, let's roll, eh?"

They all piled into the van. Somehow Patrick ended up in the copilot seat, with Claire stuck on the cooler in back. She definitely underestimated him.

Their dad started the van. "Want to know something funny?"

"Always!" Patrick said.

"Depends on the definition of funny," Claire said.

"Well, I'll let you be the judge. But you know this van? Before she became Van-Helsing, adventure seeker, she actually belonged to a dog walker."

"Really?" Claire asked.

"Oh yeah. I've never seen so much dog hair in my life. I hosed it down before I brought it home."

"There was still a lot of hair under the flooring," Patrick said.

"How...how did you get the van from the dog walker, Dad?" Claire asked.

"Ah, now that's an interesting story," he started.

Claire sighed. "Never mind." She turned away and tried to focus on the trees outside the window. She just wished her dad trusted her enough to tell her the truth about things, but if he couldn't even tell her where he got this stupid van, then—

"Remember last month when I was working all those extra hours?" he said.

Claire blinked. "Um, yeah?" she managed. "For Meredith, right?"

"I was working on this van. Meredith called me when it came in." He tapped the steering wheel proudly. "She knew I'd always wanted a van."

"Good ole Meredith," Patrick said, quoting the line their dad usually used for their old neighbor. She'd moved to the other side of town a few years ago, but she still occasionally gave their dad work in her auto mechanic shop. Even though he wasn't "technically" qualified, so she paid him in cash under the table. Sometimes too much cash; Claire remembered hearing her dad argue on the phone a few times that she'd paid him for a full day when he'd only been in the shop a few hours. But she never took money back, and eventually her dad stopped arguing. Still, on those days he'd be extra quiet, and he'd go to bed early. Like it was somehow more exhausting getting paid for work he *hadn't* done.

"Apparently a dog walker Meredith knew was looking to get out of the business, quick."

"Was there a scandal involved?" Patrick's eyes widened.

"Oh, undoubtedly. It's a cutthroat world, the world of dogs. Always being hounded."

"Dad," Claire groaned.

He grinned. "Come on, you can't blame me for that one. It was practically howling for me to use it."

"Stop. It," Claire said.

"Hey, I almost said it was a dog-eat-dog world, but that felt too obvious. Low-hanging fruit."

"You can't congratulate yourself for not saying something if you then go and say it." Claire shook her head while Patrick giggled in the front seat. "Stop laughing, it'll only encourage him."

"Fine, fine. Anyhow, this scandalous dog walker had been having some engine trouble with her Sprinter, and rather than getting it fixed, she made a deal with Meredith and just traded it in for something smaller. And then Meredith made a deal with me: if I could fix it, plus help out in the shop a few hours here and there, then she'd sell it to me cheap." He tapped his fingers against the steering wheel again. "So. That's where I was going all those hours. And that's how I got this van."

"Oh," Claire said.

"Oh is right. It's not a great story. There are no heroics. Just an old man with a sore back making it sorer."

"You're not *that* old, Dad," Patrick said.

"Thanks, son."

"You're welcome." Patrick tilted his head, his lips curling into a mischievous smile, the one that showed off both dimples and all of his teeth. "Is it true you had a pet dinosaur when you were my age?"

Their dad broke into a loud, surprised laugh. "Well played, sir."

"Chomps put me up to it." Patrick patted his stuffed animal on the head.

"Chomps isn't very kind, is he?"

"He *is* a dinosaur, Dad. He eats people." Patrick shrugged.

"Hmm, fair point." Their dad lapsed into silence as outside, the houses gradually became smaller, the yards going from jewel green to dusty brown, some of them overflowing with rusty, banged-up cars. Eventually those houses and cars were replaced by old brick buildings with shattered windows. They reminded Claire of weeping eyes and broken-toothed mouths, of old men with sore backs making them sorer.

They made her think of the steel factory back home, the one that had closed down years ago and changed everything.

She turned away from the scenery, glanced at her dad's hunched shoulders and white-knuckled hands, and knew he was thinking the same thing. "Dad? Can you tell us a story?" The words slipped out before Claire thought about them, before she even realized she was asking.

Her dad's head jerked up, eyes meeting hers in the mirror.

It was too late to take her question back, so Claire didn't bother trying. Instead, she asked, "Can you tell us about Evangeline Rose?"

CHAPTER 15

When we last left off," their dad began, "Wrong Way and his new friend, Johnny, had just ridden across the country on the fastest pair of horses in the world, ole Flash and Dash."

"I thought they were the fastest horses in all of New York," Claire said.

"If they're the fastest in the world, that would make them the fastest in New York, too," Patrick said. "Obviously."

"Listen to your brother, Claire-bear. Kid's got brains, just like his old man."

Claire sighed. This is what she got for asking for a story.

"But when they arrived in California, Edgar quickly noticed three things. The first: there was no gold lying around. The second: there were way too many people. And the third? The third thing he noticed was Evangeline Rose."

"She's not a *thing*, Dad." Claire narrowed her eyes. "And don't spend an hour telling us how beautiful she is again, either."

"I'll keep it to half an hour, tops." He chuckled.

Claire just waited him out, her face like stone.

"You know I love it when you make that face. That terrifying, soul-crushing face." He made an exaggerated shudder. "So. Moving right along . . . After our hero and his friend wandered through San Francisco for a week and determined there was no gold, Johnny became angry. 'I told you we should have just stolen the horses and been done with it,' he yelled at Edgar. 'All those weeks working, and now we've missed the gold rush!'

"'Whoa there, friend,' Edgar said calmly. 'We may have missed the gold rush, but we'll find another way to make our fortune. I promise.' And Johnny believed him. He could see that Edgar had changed on this journey, hardening like the crust of his bread, and knew he was determined to strike it rich, or die trying."

Claire shifted on her cooler seat, caught up despite herself. In front of her, Patrick leaned against the window, mouth half-open as he listened. And outside, the abandoned factories faded away, replaced by trees, their branches tangling, twining, twisting up into the sky, like fingers reaching for gold just out of reach. She closed her eyes and let her dad's words wash through her as she pictured California. For a second, she remembered that spotless condo, but then she let that go, too, and just focused on palm trees and golden beaches and impossibly large, impossibly blue skies ...

"I suppose we could try working for someone," Johnny said.

Edgar shook his head. "One thing I learned when I worked in my uncle's bakery is that you'll never get rich working for someone else. No, we need to strike out on our own. Somehow ... someway. Doing some*thing*."

Johnny grinned. "You'll have to give me more to go on, my friend."

"Excuse me," a girl said. "Do I ... know you?"

Edgar turned. A familiar girl stood before him, her strawberry blond hair curling gently around her lovely face, her eyes a deep, vivid green, her lips parted just slightly, and curved in the hint of a smile. He could have spent a good half hour describing her beauty, but in the interest of any future audiences listening to his tale, he restrained himself.

Dimly, he was aware of Johnny saying something behind him, but the words slid through his ears and back out like water trickling from an open hand. But the girl's next words stuck, and stuck hard. "Ah! You're the boy with the bread!"

Boy? Edgar ran a hand over his face. True, he'd never had much luck growing facial hair, but still, he no longer thought of himself as a *boy*. After all, he had traveled across the ocean with a pod of whales, fought off two men with a loaf of bread, and ridden all the way across this great nation in search of his fortune. But before he could argue, the girl laid a hand on his arm, and all his words, his fancy new English words, twisted together like his uncle's famous pretzel bread.

"Thank you for helping me," she said, her words as soft as her touch. "My name ... is Evangeline Rose."

"Gnnurh," Edgar managed.

Evangeline's eyebrows rose. "Interesting."

"Darling! Where have you gotten yourself off to—ah." A man stepped forward, tall, broad shouldered, and wearing an expensive hat that shadowed his ruggedly chiseled face. As soon as he saw Evangeline standing so close to Edgar, his face grew even more shadowed. "Is this man bothering you?" He pulled her behind him, tilting his chin up so Edgar could see the dangerous glint of his eyes.

Anger flashed across Evangeline Rose's lovely face and then vanished, like a duck sucked beneath the surface of a river by a hungry alligator, leaving the barest of ripples behind. Edgar was feeling quite unsettled by this strange man, and his metaphors had grown a little dark.

"I appreciate how you take such good care of me," Evangeline said, tugging her arm free. "But in this case, really, it's not needed. This is just the bread boy I told you about."

Edgar could have died right there on the spot. *Just the bread boy?*

"Ah," the man said. "Hello, bread boy. I'm Dirk Rockaford, Evangeline Rose's fiancé."

"I told you, I haven't agreed to anything yet," Evangeline Rose protested.

"Soon-to-be-fiancé," Dirk amended smoothly, confidently, "not to mention the local lawman in these here parts." He twisted so the sunlight hit the edge of his shiny badge, and made sure Edgar noticed his equally shiny pistol, tucked into his belt. "But I reckon you won't be much trouble, eh?"

"No, no trouble at all," Johnny interrupted, stepping between them. "We'll just be on our way."

"Much obliged." Dirk tipped the edge of his hat and smirked. Edgar itched to respond, but before he could, Johnny yanked him away.

Edgar spared one last glance at Evangeline Rose before Johnny pulled him around the corner and away from her.

"That gal will bring you nothing but heartbreak," Johnny said quietly. "Focus on the gold. *That's* what'll bring you happiness."

"Wise words." A woman's cool voice spoke from the shadows of a nearby saloon. Both Johnny and Edgar froze. The saloon doors swung open, and the woman stepped out into the sunlight, her hair flowing down her back in an inky river. "You boys look like you're in need of a little fame and a lot of fortune. Name's Kennedy, by the way. Ken for short."

"Ken," Johnny said approvingly. "I like your style."

"And I like your beard."

Edgar cleared his throat. "About that fame and fortune?"

Ken smiled, a dangerous smile, the kind of smile that made Edgar think of knives in the dark. "How would you feel about teaming up for a cattle drive?"

"I've heard it's the new gold rush," Johnny whispered to Edgar.

"What would we need?" Edgar asked cautiously. He wasn't sure he trusted Ken, with her princess hair and her wicked grin.

"Only what we have right here." She spread her arms wide. "An adventurous spirit, a few trusty horses, and the desire to work hard and get rich."

"Where would we go?" Edgar persisted.

"Texas."

A whole different world. "And from Texas, we would be driving the cattle to where?"

"Kansas." Ken tossed her mane of hair back and put her hands on her hips. "Most crews have at least ten men, but if there are only three of us, it means we won't have to split the profits as much. Think you can handle it?" She looked them up and down and raised her eyebrows.

"I can handle it," Johnny said immediately, puffing out his chest. "Edgar?"

Edgar hesitated. He didn't know the first thing about Ken or cattle drives or Texas, but then Ken said the words that sealed his fate: "If you do this, I'll sing your praises to my good friend."

"Your good friend?"

"I believe you've met her already." Ken's smile this time wasn't a single knife in the dark, but a whole armory. "Her name is Evangeline Rose."

"And then what happened?" Patrick asked.

"And then, er, your poor dad got a little…turned around," their dad said, looking out the window, his face scrunched with worry.

"Wait, what?" Claire sat up straighter and looked around. Rows of identical houses looked back at her, the kind with fake shutters made of plastic and painted in alternating colors.

"I was trying to find us a restroom," her dad said.

"It's called GPS, Dad," Claire said. "I'm sure it's on your phone."

"Did ole Wrong Way Jacobus use GPS?" he asked. "I don't think so."

"Maybe he should have. Then he wouldn't be stuck with a name like 'Wrong Way,'" Claire muttered.

"And deprive us of a great story?" Her dad grinned.

"Fine. Copilot." Claire pointed at Patrick. "Do your job."

"Can't. The map is under Dad's seat."

Claire sighed and dug the road atlas out.

"You touched it first!" Patrick said. "That means it's your job."

"That is so not how it works," Claire grumbled. But since her dad had been making a series of random turns for the past few minutes, she decided not to waste more time arguing. Who knew where they'd end up? Still grumbling, she flipped the pages until she found a map of Ohio, then squinted at the road numbers and did her best to navigate them.

"I feel I've earned copilot credit," she said once they were back on the highway.

"Maybe so," her dad said.

"Too bad that is so not how it works," Patrick said mockingly.

Claire resisted the urge to smack him with the battered atlas and instead idly turned the pages until she got to a map of all the major highways in the US. She found US 20 and traced their route from Ohio on to the tip of Pennsylvania, right through the middle of New York, and into Massachusetts. "Wait, we're taking Route 20, right?" she asked.

"Right-o."

Claire let that one slide. "That doesn't go near Maine."

Her dad shrugged.

"It does go to Boston, though, like you thought. We could probably just go there."

"Oh, we have to do Maine," he said.

"Why?" Claire asked.

His fingers tightened on the steering wheel. "Because . . . we have to go to the Atlantic Ocean."

"But Boston is next to the ocean." Claire watched her dad, the way his jaw muscles bunched, how intently he stared out the windshield. Like he could see their path ahead. Like he had his own plan, a plan he wasn't ready to share with them.

"But Maine is the best place to touch the ocean . . . if we want to catch a glimpse of the lost city hidden beneath its watery depths."

"There's a lost city?" Patrick breathed. "Like the ships in Lake Erie?"

"Exactly so, only twice as haunted."

Claire sighed. "That's the Lost City of Atlantis, Dad. Not Atlantic."

"There can be more than one lost city, Claire-bear," he said, his tone way too reasonable, like cities got lost all the time. "This is the lesser-known but much more fascinating Lost City of Atlanticis."

Claire groaned. "You're not even trying anymore."

"Oh, believe me, I'm trying." He grinned.

Claire shook her head. But as her dad pulled into a strip mall and parked in front of a fast-food joint, she realized her dad had accidentally told her something true: he really wanted to go to Maine. The question was, why?

CHAPTER 16

And here we are, our camp for the night!"

Claire blinked bleary eyes. She'd been half asleep, imagining men in hats and palm trees swaying in sudden wind gusts, and a woman who looked suspiciously like her dad's old friend, so it took a moment for her to realize... "A rest stop? Seriously?"

"Yep! Nice and safe here. Plus, look at that! Bathrooms, just for you, Claire-bear." He grinned.

"You're kidding, right?" Claire ran a hand through her hair. This rest area looked just like any rest area, with blazingly bright lights every few feet and several battered wooden picnic tables sitting on top of patches of dead grass. A few other cars were parked nearby, and across the parking lot loomed several giant trucks. Their drivers were probably sleeping here, too.

"Hop to it, kiddos. We've got another long day of driving ahead of us tomorrow."

Claire grabbed her toiletry kit from where it hung on a hook below the table in back. Apparently this was her life now, sleeping in rest stops like a trucker despite being a twelve-year-old girl. She sighed loudly, then sighed again, but her dad and brother ignored her, so she slipped a blank postcard out from her backpack. Ronnie would understand. Ronnie would listen.

Claire dug around in her bag, her fingers hesitating over the colored pencils, but in the end, she just grabbed a pen. "I'll get ready in a minute," she told her dad. He nodded and closed the side door, leaving her alone in the van.

Claire idly drew a few lines on the front of the postcard, thinking. What should she tell Ronnie? About the park? Julian? The quest for Maine? Maybe she could tell her about the dog walkers, the truth of the van, or—

Claire blinked. A dog stared out at her from the card, tongue lolling, ears small and pointed. She'd been doodling without realizing.

She stood up, postcard clenched in her hand. After a second's deliberation, she shoved it inside her pillowcase. She'd work on her letter later.

In the rest area bathroom she changed and brushed her teeth, then washed her face at the sink.

"Baby wipes," a woman said, passing Claire some paper towels to dry her face off.

"What?" Claire asked.

"You're in the van out back, right? The Sprinter?" The woman had short black hair and kind brown eyes, her lips a vivid red that matched her button-down shirt. It was the kind of red Ronnie would have appreciated, and Claire found herself nodding, even though she wasn't sure if she should be telling strangers she was staying in a van. "I thought so. Baby wipes are the best. Back when I lived in my truck, I always kept a packet in the door."

"You lived in your truck?" Claire gaped at her. She looked so ... normal.

The woman laughed. "Is it so hard to believe? It was a few years ago. My landlord died, rest his soul, and his son wanted me out, pronto. Jacked up the rent too high for me, and I couldn't find a place that would take me and my dog." She shrugged. "I'd rather live in my truck with my dog than give him up."

"That's terrible," Claire said.

"Eh, it wasn't all bad. A bit of a tight fit, and everything I owned was covered in dog fur, but that's nothing new. Sometimes I even kind of miss it, the freedom of it."

"Really?" Claire found that hard to believe. Would she miss traveling around in a van, too? Doubtful. "How long were you, uh ..."

"Houseless?" the woman suggested. "Six months and change."

Houseless. Claire rolled that word around in her mind, then realized the woman was staring at her.

"It *can* be a little tough," she told Claire gently, "but I got through it, and so will you."

"Oh, but I'm not—" Claire stopped. She *was* houseless. And for all she knew, it could be for six months, or maybe longer. It could be forever.

"And in the meantime, baby wipes."

"Baby wipes," Claire repeated. As she headed out into the night, she wondered how many people lived in their car or truck or van, people she wouldn't have guessed, ordinary-seeming people. Apparently it wasn't just for glamorous vanlifers and weirdos like her dad.

When she got back to the van, her dad had already set up his bed and the hammocks and was in the process of covering all the windows. Claire helped pull the curtains and put up the front window covering without a word, then crawled carefully over a sleeping Patrick, his arms wrapped around Chomps, and into her own hammock. Outside, she could hear cars pulling up, people chatting as they got out, the slam of a car door. She shifted, her hammock squeaking. A truck rattled past, then another. She shifted again. She felt strangely exposed, sleeping out here with people and cars moving past her.

"Something bothering you, Claire-bear?"

"What could possibly be bothering me? Except that I'm sleeping in a hammock, in a car, in a *rest stop* of all places."

"Not true."

"No?"

"No. This isn't a car, it's a van."

Claire clenched her hands and counted to five, then released her fists. "I'd smack you with my pillow if it wasn't such a pain in the butt to get out of this hammock."

Her dad chuckled. "I figured that would keep me safe."

Claire lay awake in her hammock a long time. More people. Someone laughing. Footsteps scraping super close to the van. "Dad?"

"Hmm?" he asked sleepily.

"Did you lock the doors?"

"Yep."

She listened to her heart, pounding, pounding, so loud her head felt like it was throbbing with that beat.

"Want me to double-check?" her dad asked after a long moment.

"Could you?" She waited for him to make a comment about troll spies or secret assassins, some story that would make her feel silly for her door-lock obsession. Instead, she heard a rustle beneath her as he got up, and then the loud *click* of the doors.

"Better?" he asked.

Claire nodded, but realized he couldn't see that. "Thanks, Dad," she whispered.

"No problem-o. Good night, Claire-bear."

Claire relaxed. And when she finally fell asleep, she dreamed of Wrong Way Jacobus and his loaf of bread, of Ken and her long princess hair, and of Evangeline Rose, whose smile was soft and sweet and reminded Claire of her mother. "No child custody sought," Evangeline Rose said, picking up a thick black marker and checking off a box.

Claire woke suddenly, completely, her heart hammering. Her hair was sticking to her face, and when she brushed it away, it felt damp. She must've been crying in her sleep.

She rolled over on her side, and something poked her in the neck, jabbing out from under her pillow. She felt around with her hand and pulled out a slightly bent postcard, the one she'd accidentally doodled on. She couldn't see it in the dark, but she brushed her thumb over the surface as if she might be able to feel the pen marks.

Maybe it was time to stop thinking about her mom and that checked box.

Claire lay there, remembering the divorce papers and how her dad had folded them smaller and smaller. She closed her eyes and pictured him folding them again, folding them until they were so small they disappeared, and her heart rate finally slowed, her body relaxing. But now that she was calm, she realized she had another problem: she really, really had to pee. She had to pee, and she was trapped in this hammock with no way out except for climbing over her brother and then stepping on her dad's head. And even then, she'd have to go outside, in the dark...

Darn her dad and his lack of van plumbing!

Claire lay there for minutes that felt like hours, until finally she gave in.

"Ow! Claire," Patrick whined.

"Ow, Claire," her dad whined next.

"See this? This is *exactly* why I wanted a bathroom in here," Claire snapped, opening the side door and slamming it behind her.

CHAPTER 17

Dear Ronnie,

I know that's oddly formal for a postcard, but if I'm sending you letters, I wanted to do it the traditional way. My dad is making fun of me, but whatever. This morning he was doing his thumb dance down the aisles of a grocery store, so what does he know, right?

We made it past Cleveland without stopping at the Natural History Museum. Dad's been complaining ever since, but I'm sure he'll get over it. Eventually. Tomorrow we're leaving Ohio and heading through Pennsylvania. We're only in it for less than fifty miles, and then on to New York. I've never been there. I keep imagining it as skyscrapers everywhere, but I know that's just the city. Dad claims the rest of it looks pretty similar to what I'm used to: lots of trees, some lakes, rolling fields. And, of course, plenty of trolls. I was hoping he'd leave them out of this, but you know how he gets.

Gotta run—I'll write again tomorrow.

Love forever,

Claire

p.s. It's supposed to be a picture of me, Dad, and Patrick in the van. In case you can't tell. I'm a little out of practice. Patrick said it looks like . . . well, I don't even want to say. But he wasn't nice about it. I swear the van has made him brattier.

p.p.s. Um, tell Mike I said hi? I mean, if you want.

"It does *not* look like a turd on wheels," Claire said as she dropped the postcard in the mail slot.

Patrick stuck his tongue out at her.

"Real mature." She shook her head. She was beginning to second-guess that p.p.s. Was it too awkward? It was. It totally was. She glanced at the mailbox, but knew it would be impossible to open it. Her letter, now dropped, was dropped forever.

"I don't have to be mature," Patrick said. "I'm eight."

"That's old enough."

"Dad's not mature either, and he's, like, a hundred."

"Watch it, Patrick," their dad said, "or I'll make you sit in the back of the turdmobile."

Claire scowled as her brother howled with laughter.

"Sorry, Claire," her dad said.

"I keep telling you, Dad. Sorry people don't smile."

His grin got even wider, and he hid it behind his hand. "Better?"

Claire sighed and walked away from him, but she could still *feel* him smiling, all the way back to their van.

Dear Ronnie,

We saw Niagara Falls! So, so epic. I tried drawing it for you, but really, you need to see it yourself. The water comes down so hard and so fast, it's white. Like permanent foam. Dad told us the first person to go over the Falls in a barrel and survive was a sixty-year-old woman, back in the 1900s. I thought he was lying, but I looked it up, and it was actually a true story, for once. Apparently she was trying to make money, but it didn't work. Dad said it never does.

I'm still not sure about this vanlife thing, but the route we're on now is kind of nice. It's all along Lake Erie, which is a lot bigger than I thought it was. We're leaving it now, though, heading out through the middle of New York. I'll tell you if it really looks the same as Michigan. From there, we'll keep going east to Maine.

Claire stopped writing and looked at her note. Her dad still hadn't said where he wanted to go after Maine. Maybe... maybe he planned to just stay. But why? What did he think he'd find all the way out there?

"Ready to roll?" her dad asked, popping his head inside the van.

"Almost." Claire quickly scribbled the rest of her note, signed it, and climbed out of the van. "Just need to drop this off."

"Hop to it, then. The open road awaits!"

"What do you think we'll do about school?" Claire asked Patrick that night as they brushed their teeth at a campground just outside Albany, New York. "We're supposed to start in a month and a half."

Patrick garbled something at her, toothpaste foam sliding out the corners of his mouth.

"Ew, gross. Spit and then talk."

He spat. "*You* asked *me* a question. You know I'm a messy toothbrusher."

"You have paste on your chin."

Patrick wiped his chin with his sleeve, then grinned at her. "Minty fresh."

Claire shook her head. "I can't believe we're related."

"Me neither." He shuddered, and she messed up his hair. "And I don't mind skipping school," he added, swatting her hand away.

Claire frowned. "We can't. There are laws and things."

"Homeschooling?"

Her stomach dropped. No way her dad wanted to home-school them. "Or maybe," she said, testing out her theory, "he wants to live in Maine."

"Nah," Patrick said, completely dismissive.

Claire wanted to argue more, but she was afraid Patrick would bring out his *own* theory, that they were on some kind of rescue mission for their mom.

"Anyhow, I like life on the road," Patrick said.

"You might not like it after another week. Or a month. Or a year."

"Or I might," he said. "And you might, too."

Claire shook her head.

"You *might*," he repeated, jabbing her in the shoulder with his wet toothbrush.

"Ew, don't touch me with that."

He held it up like a sword, grinning.

"Don't," Claire warned, backing up.

"Or what?" He took a step, then another.

She uncapped the toothpaste, and he froze in place. "Yeah, that's what I thought."

"Fine. Truce for now."

Claire nodded solemnly. "Truce for now."

They walked back to the van, the trees swaying above them. There were a few other families camping down the road, some with super-elaborate setups: pop-up shade tents, fancy hammock stands, the full REI catalog. But even those people seemed envious of their van. Claire hated to admit it, but it made her feel almost...proud.

"You know, I like *you* better on the road, too," Patrick decided.

Claire stopped. "What?"

"You're funner." He scrunched his face. "More fun," he self-corrected. "At least, for you."

Before Claire could think of a response, he sprinted ahead.

CHAPTER 18

Dear Ronnie,

We finally made it to Maine! We stopped in Portland, which is right on the coast, and not at all what I was picturing. My dad took us onto the roof of a bowling alley where there was this giant Airstream—it's a camper that's all metal, kind of ugly if you ask me, but people seem to really love them for some reason. I bet if you ask Mike, he'll tell you all about them.

Anyhow. On the roof was this Airstream, only instead of a camper, it had been converted into a taco truck. We met this old couple there whose car Dad had fixed for free years ago, or something like that. They kept going on and on about how he was a lifesaver, and they bought us our tacos—I had a cauliflower one, just to gross out Patrick, but it was actually really good—and then Dad went off with them to the bar, and we got to watch a movie on this giant screen. On the roof!

When Dad came back he was super weird and quiet. But then he told us that he and Mom came to this place for their honeymoon, so maybe he was just sad? Also how bizarre is it that he took us to their honeymoon spot? Did I tell you Patrick thinks we're going to rescue her? I never told him about . . . you know. What we found. But I shouldn't have to tell him. Dad should tell him. And it doesn't matter, because this has nothing to do with her. But still. Weird that we came here.

Love forever,

Claire

p.s. I drew the Airstream for you on the front. I'm starting to get better. Patrick didn't make fun of it, at least.

"Where should we sleep tonight?" their dad asked Claire after she dropped off her letter.

"You don't have a plan?" Claire asked, surprised.

"My plans kind of . . . fell through a little," he admitted.

They were still in Portland, parked next to the post office, their windows rolled all the way down. Outside, the edges of the sky deepened into a rich navy blue, the buildings in the distance transforming into cutout silhouettes as the sun crept its way down behind them. Claire thought she could smell the ocean ahead, all salty and wind-tossed, and for a second she wanted to park right by it, sleep with the windows down and the breeze filling their van all night.

She remembered that sign her dad had bought, about sleeping in his vehicle and waking up in the neighborhood of his choice. For the first time, she almost understood it. "Can we go see the ocean?" she blurted.

"What?"

"The Atlantic Ocean. Wasn't that why we came here?"

Her dad grinned. "That is one hundred percent why we came here, to track down the Lost City of Atlanticis. Or, barring that, to at least get our feet good and wet." He glanced up at the sky. "Not sure how much time we'll have today, though…"

"It's not dark yet," Claire said.

His eyes widened. "Are you, my reasonable child, advocating for a late-evening oceanside visit?"

Claire hesitated. It felt like a trap. "Maybe," she hedged.

"Well then, I guess maybe there's enough time. If we hurry."

"Woo hoo! Lost city!" Patrick pumped his fist in the air as their dad started up the van, the purr of the diesel engine vibrating beneath them.

They drove to Portland Head Light, which their dad claimed was one of the most photographed lighthouses in the world, and for once Claire believed him. And even though the nearby beach was rocky, and not sandy like she'd imagined, she loved clambering down to the water and sticking her feet in, while Patrick claimed he saw a city hidden beneath every wave. Finally, though, it grew so dark their dad made them head back.

"We still need to find a place to bunk for the night," he said, shooing them over the rocks to their van, where they wiped down their feet and brushed their teeth, right there in the parking lot. "Hit up those outhouses, too, just in case."

"In case of what?" Claire asked, but her dad wouldn't say. She and Patrick exchanged nervous looks and didn't argue.

Afterward, Claire stared out the side window at the stars as her dad looked up places on his phone. She tried not to feel anxious—of course he'd find somewhere for them to sleep—but as the minutes ticked by, her heart seemed to speed up, until she could feel it thumping hard against her chest like it was a clock.

"All the campgrounds are full," he said, finally putting down his phone. "I think we might just have to wing it."

"Wing it?" Claire swallowed, her mouth going dry. "What does that mean?" Her dad and the words "wing it" were *not* a very comforting combination.

"We-ell," he drawled, "it means we might be in for a long, boring night, or an adventure. No way to know!" He grinned, but his smile fell away at the look on Claire's face. "How about we try sleeping here. What do you think?"

Claire looked across the parking lot at the "no overnight camping" signs posted. It was too dark to read them now, but she could feel them looming there, practically screaming.

"Or," her dad said, following her gaze, "we can try to find somewhere else."

"There aren't any rest areas?" Claire asked.

"Well, there might be ... but Maine doesn't allow overnight camping in their rest areas."

"Why not?" Patrick asked. "Isn't *resting* what a rest area is for?"

"Yeah, isn't it dangerous to force tired drivers onto the road?" Claire added. It felt like the night was closing in on them, all dark and creepy. The lighthouse flashed in the distance, illuminating stretches of inky water, while the waves beat against the shore in loud, angry bursts.

Their dad held up his hands. "I'm not arguing with either of you. I don't think it makes sense, either, but it's their rule."

"I thought you didn't care about rules," Claire grumbled.

"Oh, I don't, not usually, but—" He broke off suddenly, looking out the driver-side window as a van pulled up next to them. "Just a second, kids," he said, his voice tense. Claire clasped her hands together tightly and waited. Were they in trouble? Or ... what if this person was a robber? Or a serial killer? Or—

Her dad opened his door. "Wait, Dad, what are you doing?" Claire cried, but it was too late; he'd gotten out and was walking over to the other van.

The passenger-side window rolled down and a woman stuck her head out, her long gray hair whipping around her face in the wind. "Howdy, friend," she said cheerfully. "You look a little lost. Need any help?"

"Oh, I think I'm doing just fine, thanks," Claire's dad said.

"Are you sure? You sleeping in that?" The woman pointed at Van-Helsing.

Claire watched her dad nod once, slowly.

"Nice! Always wanted a Sprinter, but Tracy here was all about the classic VW."

"Still am!" the other person in the van said. "And always will be."

"Anyhow," the first woman continued, "we've been kicking around this part of Maine for a little while, and it's not the easiest place to boondock. But there's a hunting and outdoor recreation store that lets people camp in their parking lot. Not the most glamorous, but it's pretty safe, well-lit. Here's the address." She handed him a slip of paper. "We're not going that way, but we can, if you need us to show you."

"Julie," Tracy said.

"What? This poor man might need our help." She smiled. "We're both retired, see. Plenty of time."

"Ah, well, I should be able to find it on my own. No need to put yourselves out, but thank you."

"Anytime, my fellow tumbleweed. Anytime." Julie waved once, then rolled up her window and the van drove slowly away.

"Tumbleweed, eh?" Her dad smiled as he climbed back into the van.

"You love that, don't you?" Claire shook her head.

"You know it. Now, let's go check out this parking lot. Sure sounds like a good time to me!"

"What's boondocking?" Patrick asked as they pulled out.

"Not sure, but it sounds exciting, whatever it is."

Claire squeezed her hands as she listened to her brother and dad chatter in the front. She had almost—almost—started to like this life. She'd even gotten a little bit comfortable in the van, with the driving and the sleeping in different places. But it was dangerous. If she wasn't careful, she'd be all hashtag vanlifing, and then next thing she knew, she'd forget that this wasn't normal at all. And if she forgot that, then there'd be no one holding on to normal, and who knew where her family would end up.

Because that's what tumbleweeds did. They just blew and blew and blew forever until they eventually crumbled and fell apart.

CHAPTER 19

Dear Ronnie,

I wish you could write me back. This feels very one-sided, and I have so much to tell you. We were in Maine for a few days. Dad was super weird the whole time. I mean, even for him, and that's really saying something. But then all of a sudden he decided we needed to check out part of the Appalachian Trail, so here we are now in Roanoke, Virginia, where he's gotten really into boondocking.

Basically we brush our teeth and get dressed for bed, then set up our van for the night and put up all the blinds except for the one over the windshield, obviously. After that we drive until we find a good spot, like, on a street where there are other cars parked, or once we parked outside a coffee shop that had other Sprinter vans out front. And then we slide into place, silent, like a shark.

That's how dad describes it. Patrick, as you can imagine, loves it. I'm guessing Mike would love that, too. Or maybe not. And as for me, I do NOT love it, because, first, I don't know if it's legal, even though Dad says it totally is, and second, if I wake up in the middle of the night and have to pee, I'm stuck holding it, so I don't drink any water after noon unless Dad notices and makes me—he doesn't want me dehydrated. He just doesn't get it.

This is getting long. Tomorrow we're hiking . . . wish me luck!

Love love love,

Claire

Dear Ronnie,

So, yeah, Appalachian Trail. We were out there All. Day. All day! My legs are dead. Actually, everything hurts.

I guess there's a family who brought their kids, who were eight and eleven, across the entire two-thousand-mile trail. I didn't believe Dad when he told me that, but he showed me a book about it. Then he suggested we write a book about our van trip. I told him I'd write it and call it "Hashtag Van Lie" and he laughed so hard I thought he might choke. Then I think he cried a little, because he's pretty sore, too.

But the trail really was beautiful. You would have loved it. I think even Mike would like it, even though he's not much of a hiker. I loved it, too, for a few hours, and then it felt like all those green mountains were just taunting me. Still, we got to this place called Tinker Cliffs, and it felt like we were standing on the cracks at the edge of the world, with these windswept little trees near us, and then out in the distance all these folds and folds of mountains, turning from green to blue to purple as they overlapped in the distance, and . . . and I can't even describe it. So I drew it for you.

And yes, that's me pushing Patrick off the cliff, but he totally deserves that. The drawing, not the actual death. He's been obnoxious this whole time. Kept jumping around, claiming he was fighting the snipes.

Wish you were here with me.

Love,

Claire

Dear Ronnie,

We're currently parked in a Walmart parking lot near Lexington, Kentucky. Yep, that's where we're sleeping tonight. And here you thought this would be a Grand Adventure. A parking lot. In front of Walmart. Ugh. NOT FUN.

Sorry I couldn't think of something good to draw. You just get a sad face.

Xoxo,

Claire

"A sad face?" Patrick whispered.

"Appropriate, right?" Claire whispered back.

"Why do you keep talking about Mike?" Patrick asked.

"What?" Claire blinked. They were sitting on their dad's bed converted into a couch and using the table Patrick had so proudly helped sand, while their dad talked to someone on the phone up front.

"Stop leering over my shoulder." Claire shoved her brother. "And I'm not."

"You are. Every postcard you mention him."

"Why are you reading my postcards?" Claire could feel her face burning. She hadn't been talking about Mike that much, right?

"I like seeing your drawings."

"Oh." Now Claire's whole body felt warm. "Really?"

"They're definitely getting better."

"Thanks. I think."

Their dad hung up the phone. "Sorry about that, kiddos." He looked worn around the edges, like even he wasn't having a Grand Adventure.

"Everything okay?" Claire asked.

"Okay? Are you kidding me? Everything is fantabulous!"

Claire winced.

"You don't like that one, either?"

"It's not 'one,' Dad," Claire said. "That's the whole problem. You took two innocent words and mashed them cruelly together."

"They're better combined," Patrick chimed in. "Everyone knows that."

"Yeah, Claire," her dad said. "Everyone knows that." He grinned, but she could see his neck muscles straining. "Now, I know this isn't the most exciting place to spend a night, but... you know what is exciting?" He waited a beat. "Ice cream!"

Patrick sat up so straight it was like he'd been turned to wood, his blue eyes wide and excited. "Ice cream?" he said.

"You scream?" their dad said. They both looked at Claire. "If you want it, you've got to say it, Claire-bear."

She sighed, but she really did want ice cream. It was hot in the van, fan or no. "We all scream," she muttered.

"For ice cream!" her dad and brother finished.

"Now, let's go get some!" Her dad's smile this time looked a little less forced, and as Claire followed him out of the van and into the store, she tried not to worry about their next destination, and the one after that.

CHAPTER 20

Dear Ronnie,

Happy happy birthday! I wish I was there with you. We're in Kansas, and it's so hot here, and Dad has been trying to stop at places with showers along the way, but I never feel as clean using a public shower, you know? It's like those gross showers at the pool, the ones where you don't want to take off your flip-flops because the tile is all mildewy and you can just imagine the germs collecting. Picture that, and then imagine those are the only showers you ever get, and you'll understand how it's been.

We stopped in Kansas City yesterday. There was some confusion because Dad was trying to take us to the one in Kansas, but we ended up at the one in Missouri instead. What a silly thing to name a Missouri city, right? But since we were there, we went to Union Station so Patrick could see the trains, and there's lots of cool things there. Even a planetarium. I guess I *still like those. A bit. We're in Wichita now, outside the Great Plains Transportation Museum, because Patrick is back on his train kick. You remember how last year he decided he was a train? I'm afraid I'll be dealing with that all over again. Ugh.*

Are you having a big party? Dad says you can call me on his cell phone. We'll be in service most of the day. Probably for the next few days. You know you can always call. Please call. I miss you.

Gotta run. I'll write more tomorrow.

Sending birthday love,

Claire

Claire looked over her letter. She hadn't mentioned Mike once. Ha! *So there, Patrick,* she thought. She still wasn't sure how she felt about Mike, but she knew she'd handled his confession badly. Just thinking about it made her want to shrivel up and die, so she tried not to.

Instead, she thought of Ronnie, and her birthday, and how much fun she would probably be having without her. Her stomach lurched, and she clenched her fists. The postcard crumpled. "Oh no!" Claire quickly smoothed it out on top of the table. "Sorry, Ronnie," she whispered.

Not that Ronnie would notice a few wrinkles. She'd be too distracted with all her other friends, and birthday cake, and presents. Claire could practically smell that mix of sunscreen and chlorine and cake that always went along with

Ronnie's birthday, the one day a year Ronnie's mom let her eat as many grams of sugar as she wanted. Ronnie always saved the "ica" part of the icing for Claire, since her mom also insisted on writing her full name, Veronica.

Someone else would eat those letters this time. Probably Jessica, who already made comments every year about how they matched up better with her name. Ugh. Jessica and her high-pitched laugh and her need to tell everyone the price of literally every single item of clothing she ever wore. And even worse than that, she'd been trying to be best friends with Ronnie for years. Now she'd have her chance.

Claire's eyes burned. She didn't even like the taste of icing that much. She just ate it because Ronnie liked it. It wasn't such a big deal to miss it this year. Or next.

She sniffed, then sniffed again.

It wasn't a big deal.

The van side door opened, and her dad poked his head in. "You'd better hurry with your letter," he said. "I think your brother is trying to leave us to become a train conductor."

"Really?"

"Don't look so excited. You'd miss him, and you know it."

Claire thought about it. "I guess," she sighed.

"Let's go get him and drag him home, eh?"

Claire put down her pencil and hopped out of the van.

Her dad closed the door behind her. "Like chicken?" He held out his arm. "Then grab a wing."

"Oh, Dad." Claire shook her head, but she looped her arm through his anyway.

Dear Ronnie,

Ugh, I was right about Patrick. He's been making train noises ever since we left Kansas a few days ago. I was hoping you'd call so I could tell you about it, but I guess you're busy. Me too. We're doing a lot of driving today, so I'll write more later. If I can.

Love,

Claire

The next day, Ronnie still hadn't called. "You could call her, too, you know," Claire's dad said. "I know you have her number memorized."

Claire shrugged. "If she wants to talk, she'll call me first." Because if Ronnie *didn't* call, that meant she didn't miss Claire anymore.

And what if Claire did call, and Ronnie didn't answer? Her heart ached, just imagining it, the phone ringing on and on and on. Ronnie's mom answering, calling for Ronnie, and then saying, "Sorry, Claire, she's busy right now. She's out having so much fun with Jessica. Two peas in a pod, those girls, the absolute best of friends you ever saw. She'll have to call you later, if she remembers." And then the *click* of the receiver, the long *buzz* of the dead line, and silence.

And then Claire would know Ronnie really had moved on, and she'd already been forgotten.

Claire didn't write a postcard that day. Or the next. Or the day after. She kept waiting for Ronnie to call first, but Ronnie never did.

CHAPTER 21

Claire never slept well when they boondocked. Her dad always claimed it was fine. "It's like stealth mode," he explained, "only more stationary." Claire knew they weren't hurting anyone; they never left behind garbage and they were super quiet. But still, imagining all those people sleeping in their comfortable homes while she lurked outside in a big white van made her very uncomfortable.

Which was why she was awake when the first knock sounded at their van door.

Claire froze, every muscle tense. Maybe she'd imagined it.

Another knock, this time followed by a soft "Hello?" and then the beam of a flashlight shining through their curtains. "Anyone in there?"

Claire turned her head a fraction. She could see the whites of Patrick's eyes in the dim light. "Dad?" she breathed.

"Shh," her dad whispered.

"Hello? It's the police."

The police. Icy dread washed over Claire. She knew this was illegal! What were the police going to do to them? Throw them in jail? Bust down their door and drag them out into the street?

"Dad?" she whispered.

"Shh, shh," he repeated.

Knock-knock-knock. "Is anyone in here?" the officer's voice repeated, and Claire couldn't stop herself. He was a cop. You weren't supposed to ignore the law.

"Dad," Claire squeaked.

Her dad sighed. "I know, Claire-bear. I understand." And she knew that what he really meant was, "I understand how you are." It made her feel both ashamed and strangely loved as he sat up and opened the side door.

Claire listened to him talk to the officer, her heart hammering so hard she caught only snippets of words. Things like, "can't sleep overnight here" and "old logging road." Her dad made approving noises, asked a few questions about directions, and then a few minutes later it was over. He closed the side door, yawned, and stretched.

"Grab your seats, kiddos. We're changing venues."

* * *

"I bet there are thousands of snipes in these woods," Patrick whispered as they pulled up to the old logging road the cop had told them they could use for camping. Temporarily, at least.

"I thought snipes only traveled through pipes," Claire said.

"Yes, but they *live* in trees. Obviously. Right, Dad?"

"Right, son."

"I'm more worried about bears, or mountain lions," Claire said. Who knew Colorado had so many trees? Claire had always pictured it as a land of sweeping rocky mountains. "Or..." she stopped, noticing the van up ahead. A Sprinter, just like theirs, only this one was bigger, newer, and painted a charcoal gray. She remembered how Mike had described their van as *sleek*. This one was sleek times a hundred, which made it look another word, *dangerous*. "Or serial killers," she finished.

Her dad pulled up on the side of the road near the other van.

"Dad, maybe we should keep driving," Claire said.

"Honey, your old man is very tired." He rubbed his eyes, then scrubbed a hand down his face for emphasis. He *did* look tired. There were patches of stubble on his chin—the closest her dad ever got to growing a beard—and his eyes were red-rimmed and bloodshot. "I think serial killers are probably safer than my driving right now."

Claire bit her lip. She eyed the van looming in front of them, barely visible in the night.

"They're probably all sleeping anyhow." He turned off their van.

Without the diesel engine rumbling, it felt like he'd suddenly turned up the night. An owl calling in the distance, crickets, the wind, tree branches creaking... Claire heard them all in stereo, and she realized something terrible. "I have to pee," she whispered.

"Plenty of trees for you to pick from."

"Wait, what?" Claire peered at her dad. He wasn't joking. "You want me to pee behind a *tree*? Like an *animal*?"

"Technically, you are an animal, Claire-*bear*." He grinned. "Take a walk on the wild side."

"You are *so* not funny."

"No, he's pretty funny," Patrick said.

"Thanks, son."

"You're welcome, Dad." They did that annoying fist bump thing, and for one second, just one brief, teeny-tiny second, Claire missed her mother so intensely, it felt like her whole body throbbed with one single thought: *I wish she was here.* Because she'd understand. She wouldn't tell her daughter to pee in the woods. In fact, if she were with them, they'd have put a bathroom into the van, limited space or no, with a toilet *and* a shower.

Claire knew, even as she thought it, that she was being ridiculous. She had no idea what her mom would have wanted, or what she'd have done. She didn't really know her mother at all. All she had were images of other people's mothers, like Ronnie's mom, who would never have agreed to move into a van in the first place.

"You might not realize this," Claire said carefully through gritted teeth, "but it's a little different for a girl. I can't just, just pee, okay?"

Her dad shrugged. "Honey-bear—"

"Don't even."

He laughed. "Fine. Claire. My sweet-tempered, gentle flower of a daughter. We're staying here for the night. So you have a choice: go find a nice tree, or hold it."

"I'll hold it."

"Okay then." He put up the windshield and side-door coverings, drew the curtains on the other windows, and fixed the blankets on his bed, Patrick cheerfully helping him. Claire stood as far to the side as she could, her fingers curled tight into fists.

By the time he was done, though, she'd made up her mind. "Fine," she muttered.

Her dad looked over. "What's that?"

Heidi Lang

"I'm going to find a tree."

He grinned. "That's the spirit."

"I'll go with you, Claire," Patrick said. "I have to pee, too."

Claire was embarrassed by how relieved that made her feel, that she wouldn't have to go out into the woods at night alone. Still, she didn't want Patrick to know that. "Fine," she said. "As long as you don't look."

"Ew. Why would I look?" He opened the side door and hopped out, and Claire followed him.

"Pack it in, pack it out," their dad said, handing Claire some toilet paper and a ziplock bag.

"What?"

"No littering, so used tp goes in the bag, and we'll toss it when we find a garbage can."

Claire glared at him. "You are not my favorite person right now."

He put a hand to his heart, like she'd shot him. "You wound me."

Sighing, Claire took the supplies and followed her brother through the trees. The moon was half full and beautiful, stars winking around it. It made her miss her room. Were the new owners painting over her ceiling? Or maybe they had a kid who would leave it just as it was, who would appreciate it. She hoped so.

"Hurry up," Patrick whispered as Claire found a tree.

166

"I'm trying. Don't talk to me." Her brother had his back turned, but Claire still moved a few more trees away. Her skin prickled, and she was hyperaware of every little sound, of the cool night air, of insects buzzing way too close. This was horrible. How did people ever survive without indoor plumbing? She'd never take it for granted again.

"Claire?" Patrick called.

"Almost done."

"I think there's someone else out here."

Claire's heart stopped. She put a hand against the tree in front of her, pressing her palm hard into the rough bark so she wouldn't fall over.

"Claire?" Patrick called again, his voice quavering.

"I'm coming." She finished up and hurried over, crunching through fallen leaves, her footsteps way too loud. The crickets had gone silent, as if the forest was waiting for something to happen, and she couldn't help imagining every single horror movie her dad had ever let her watch. The skin between her shoulder blades tightened, and when she spun, she was sure something had moved right behind her. She peered at the spot, but it was too dark to see anything. Just a shadow under the trees?

"Let's get back," Patrick whispered, glancing all around. They hadn't gone too far from the van, and it only took a few seconds before it came into view.

Claire glanced instinctively at the dark van parked in front of theirs.

The doors were open.

She caught her breath. Voices up ahead. She didn't know when it happened, or who'd reached for whom, but somehow she and Patrick were holding hands as they stepped out of the woods.

"And there they are!" her dad said, beaming in the light spilling from inside their van, not looking sleepy at all. "Claire, Patrick, this is Celeste—"

An extremely slender woman with frizzy blond hair braided in a ring around her head smiled over at them.

"—Peter—" Next to Celeste loomed a tall, broad-shouldered man with short dark hair and a very bushy beard that hung halfway down his chest.

"—and Justin." A boy stepped forward. Claire guessed he was about her age, maybe a little older, tall and slender like his mom, with tousled brown hair and light eyes, and when he smiled at her, the left corner of his mouth quirked higher than the right. Her heart beat so fast she felt dizzy. She dropped Patrick's hand immediately.

"Call me P-Sign," Peter said, holding up his hand, two fingers extended in a vee. Claire noticed he was wearing a tie-dyed T-shirt, all reds and yellows and pinks. Claire had to look at him and Celeste, these strange adults, because she felt like she couldn't look at Justin. Mostly because she *wanted* to look at Justin.

"He has the spirit of the sixties in his soul," Celeste said, her voice a pleasant husky rasp, like she had a bad cold.

Claire nodded, even though she wasn't quite sure what that meant. "Oh," she murmured, finally looking Justin in the eyes. His smile widened, and she knew whatever Celeste had said, it didn't matter, because nothing could ruin this one beautiful, perfect moment—

"Hey, um, Claire," Patrick said.

Claire tore her eyes away from the new boy. "What?"

"You dropped your pee bag." Patrick held out the ziplock bag, pinched carefully between the tips of his thumb and forefinger.

—except for her brother.

CHAPTER 22

Y ou don't sleep in the van?" Claire asked, watching Justin set up his hammock for the night in the nearby forest. She was wide awake now, and not at all scared of the dark. The crickets sang, the trees danced in the breeze, and the stars overhead were extra bright.

"Not if I can help it," Justin said. "I mean, our van is super cool, of course. I helped my parents convert it and everything. But this"—he shook his hammock—"is way better, you know?"

"What about bugs?"

"They're no big deal."

"So, bugs don't bug you." Claire wanted to swallow those words back immediately, she was so embarrassed. It was something her dad might have said. What was wrong with her? "Sorry, I—"

"Don't be sorry. You're funny." Justin grinned at her, a lock of hair trailing into his eye.

"Me?" Claire flushed. *Was* she funny? Her dad seemed to think so, but he was a weirdo. But if Justin thought so, maybe it was true. "Um, thanks." She dragged her gaze past him and studied his hammock. It had some kind of strange netting on top of it. "What's that?"

"Oh." He dropped his smile. "Well, that's a bug net. You know, just in case."

"Oh," Claire said.

"Some places are super buggy," he added, a little defensively.

"I get it," Claire said quickly, and she was rewarded with his smile again.

"I thought you would." The way he said it made Claire feel special, like she was not only funny, but the kind of girl who'd understand about bug nets and hammocks and sleeping outdoors. Someone strong and brave. Someone like Ronnie.

She pictured her friend, with her deep, confident voice, how athletic she was, how pretty. If Ronnie were there, Claire would fade into her shadow, and Justin would never notice her. Without her friend around, maybe *Claire* could be the confident one instead, funny and cool, the kind of girl Justin would like.

For the first time ever, she was glad Ronnie wasn't there.

That thought made her falter. Was she already changing, becoming this other person? The kind of person who didn't mind leaving people behind?

A person like her mother.

"You okay?" Justin asked.

Claire nodded. "I'm fine." And she was. She hadn't left Ronnie behind. She'd written her, again and again, and Ronnie hadn't even bothered to call her.

"Long day on the road, am I right?" Justin swept his hair back from his face.

"You know it," Claire said. And then she uttered the two words she swore she'd never, ever say: "Hashtag vanlife."

Justin burst out laughing. "Hashtag vanlife," he agreed. "You know, I'm really glad you're camping with us. See you tomorrow?"

Claire grinned, her insides warm and fuzzy. "I hope so." She waved good night, and then walked back to her van, still grinning.

"What's wrong with your face?" Patrick asked.

Claire ignored him. She was still mad about that whole pee bag incident. It was like he was *trying* to embarrass her, but it didn't matter, because Justin thought she was funny and wanted to see her tomorrow.

"So, kids," their dad said as he joined them in the van, closing the side door behind him, "Celeste has invited us to caravan with them tomorrow. They're heading to Gunnison National Forest. I guess there's dispersed camping available there."

"What's that?" Claire asked.

"Places you can camp for free." He winked. "My favorite. And probably full of all kinds of trolls, this being Colorado and all." He nudged Patrick, who for once didn't take the bait.

"And we'd be camping with Celeste, and, um, and her family?" Claire couldn't make herself say Justin's name. Not in front of her dad.

"If we decide to join them."

"Can we? Please?" Claire begged.

"I thought you might be interested. But I gotta warn you, it's rough camping. That means probably no toilets, and definitely no showers. You sure you want to?"

Claire nodded.

"Patrick?"

He shrugged. "I'd rather it just be us, Dad."

Their dad frowned. "Hmm. Generally I would, too, son. But Celeste and Peter have been telling me about their hashtag vanlife posts, and how they're using them to fund their trip, and I gotta say, I'm a little curious to learn more. But only if you're okay with it."

Patrick sighed. "I guess it's okay. Just for tomorrow, though, right?"

Their dad hesitated. "Well, they also told me about a vanlife rally. They're heading in that direction, and I thought maybe we'd go there, too."

Patrick sighed again.

"How about we see how tomorrow goes, and then we decide, eh?"

"Okay," Patrick said reluctantly.

As Claire climbed up into her hammock, she tried to imagine what it would be like to sleep outside, listening to animals rustling in the woods instead of the sounds of her dad snoring and Patrick shifting and the van creaking. And even though she thought it would be cool to be the kind of person who did that, she knew that secretly, she was pretty happy inside the van.

Claire drifted to sleep with that thought filling her: she was actually happy sleeping in a van. Maybe she really *was* a tumbleweed.

Maybe she could be like Justin after all.

Claire was dirty, and sweaty, and trying not to care. But as the sweat stuck her shirt to her back and the dirt itched down her legs, the knowledge that there would be no shower waiting at the end of this hike pressed against her more fiercely than the humidity of the day. And just how long *was* this trail? They'd been hiking out here for over an hour.

"Isn't hiking the greatest?" Justin asked, looking especially cute in gray cargo shorts and a button-down green shirt as he walked next to her. He could have been an athletic-wear model, and Claire couldn't bring herself to say anything about the dirt and bugs and heat. Not when he was looking at her like she must be the kind of girl who would be totally into it.

She plastered a grin on her face. "Hiking sure is… something, alright," she managed.

It was enough for Justin, who grinned back at her, like they were sharing some sort of secret.

"Claire hates hiking," Patrick spoke up.

Claire scowled at him. "Don't you have someone else you can bother?" Up ahead, she could hear her dad laugh as he hiked along with Celeste and P-Sign. Why couldn't Patrick hike with them?

"No," Patrick said. "They're being boring up there. They keep talking about those stupid vanlife videos."

Justin stiffened. "They're not stupid."

"Yeah, Patrick," Claire said, shooting him a look. "They're not."

Patrick shrugged. "They seem pretty stupid to me. I told your mom," he pointed at Justin, "that I didn't want to be in her video, but she still keeps talking and talking about it."

"She wants you to be in one of *our* videos?" Justin's eyebrows drew together.

Patrick shrugged again. "Guess so."

"Huh." Justin kicked a rock. "Cool, I guess." But he looked annoyed.

"We hiked part of the Appalachian Trail last week," Claire blurted, then immediately regretted it. Why was she still talking about hiking?

"Oh yeah?" Justin brightened. "I'm planning on hiking the whole thing someday. All two thousand two hundred miles. I think it would be such an experience, you know?"

"Definitely." She remembered how tired she'd been after one day of hiking those hills, and tried to imagine months of that. It would be an experience for sure, and not one she'd really want. But she could totally picture Justin out there, hiking all day, sleeping in his hammock at night, feeling completely at home with it.

"Maybe we could hike it together someday." He nudged her shoulder.

"Yeah, maybe," Claire said.

Patrick made a gagging noise, and she turned to see him miming putting his finger down his throat. She thought Justin might be annoyed with that, too, but he just laughed.

They turned a corner and found all the parents waiting for them just up ahead. "Don't worry, we're practically back to our campsite now," Claire's dad said, winking at her.

"I wasn't worried," Claire said quickly.

"Claire loves hiking now." Patrick rolled his eyes.

"Oh yeah?" Her dad beamed, and Claire could imagine all the miles and miles of hiking he was planning for her future. She was so going to kill Patrick.

"See what I mean?" Celeste said, swooping in and pinching Patrick's cheeks. "Just look at this cute little face. He'd be a perfect addition to our videos."

Claire would have felt bad for her brother, except this probably served him right for being so obnoxious.

"Not sure he'd be a willing addition, though," her dad said, and even though he sounded calm, there was something under his words, a jaggedness, that Celeste must have picked up on. She let Patrick go.

"So, Justin, I hear you're into rock climbing," Claire's dad said abruptly.

Justin blinked, tearing his eyes away from Patrick. "Oh, yes. Very into it."

"I did my fair share of bouldering back in my younger days," Claire's dad said. "Never did try roping in, though. Thinking I might take it up again eventually."

"Really?" Justin fell into step next to him, getting caught up in a discussion about bouldering techniques and best places to climb. As they rounded the trail into their campsite, Claire let Justin drift away from her. It wasn't surprising to lose him to her dad.

She trudged back to her van, trying not to feel disappointed. Sighing, she rummaged around for her baby wipes, then sat in the open side door and looked outside, absently swatting the occasional bug and wiping halfheartedly at the dirt on her ankles.

"Hey!" Justin called.

Claire looked up.

He jogged toward her, brown hair tousled. "There you are! Can I sit next to you?"

Claire shifted over to give him space.

"Why'd you run off?" he asked.

"I guess I figured you'd be talking to my dad for a while."

He shrugged. "Your dad is interesting and all, but I'd much rather talk to you."

Claire blinked. "R-really?"

"Definitely. I mean, no offense, but your dad kind of talks a lot, you know?"

Claire laughed. "Oh, I know, trust me."

"I like how you listen to me." And he gave her that crooked smile, the one that made her heart race, and she finally understood why Edgar had said, "Gnnurh," when Evangeline Rose touched his arm and told him her name.

As he launched into his next story, she tried to focus on it, but the whole time she could hear him saying how he'd rather talk to her. He'd choose her over her dad. He liked her.

"Right?" he asked a few minutes later, and she nodded.

"Yeah. Definitely." She wasn't sure what she was agreeing to, but it didn't really matter.

CHAPTER 23

Claire looked out the window at the beautiful trees while her mind kept conjuring up images of Justin, with his crooked smile and his perfect hazel eyes, and those freckles, the way he said her name. She sighed. She missed him already. Which was ridiculous, since she'd see him when they got to the next campsite.

Claire sighed again.

"Whole lot of sighing going on there," her dad remarked. "Sounds like someone could use a good story." He glanced in the rearview mirror. "How about it, Patrick? Want to hear a story?"

Patrick shrugged. He'd been quiet since they told Celeste they'd keep traveling with her and her family, his disapproval radiating out in silent spirals.

"Or I could sing?"

"Story," Claire and Patrick said immediately.

"Want to hear more about ole Wrong Way? It's been a little while since we last checked in with him."

Not since before Maine, Claire realized. Her dad had barely told any stories at all since then, which was very unlike him.

"Well?" he asked.

"Sure," Claire said quickly. "Wrong Way story."

"Patrick?"

"I guess so," Patrick mumbled.

"Come on, show a little enthusiasm. This is your ancestor, your blood!"

"If you say so." Patrick looked out the window.

"You are a tough crowd." Their dad pretended to loosen his collar. "But I've had tougher. Did I tell you kids about the time I had to perform in front of an ant colony?"

"Dad, seriously?" Claire groaned. Clearly her dad's storytelling drive had returned with a vengeance.

"An ant colony?" Patrick chewed his lip thoughtfully.

"Oh yes. You see, I'd fallen asleep, and when I woke up, I was surrounded, all these tiny red and black—"

"Dad!" Claire said. "Focus. Wrong Way Jacobus. Let's stick to one story at a time, okay?"

He grinned. "Fine. Wrong Way Jacobus." He cleared his throat. "Last time we left Edgar, he was heading out on a cattle drive with Johnny and their new mysterious friend, Ken."

"Wait, what about Evangeline Rose?" Claire asked. "Did Edgar just leave her behind?"

"He had no choice. He couldn't exactly sweep her off her feet with only one measly breadstick to his name."

"Not all women care about money," Claire said. She thought of Justin, who lived in a van. She'd stay in a van for him. Then she thought of how she'd had to pee in the woods twice yesterday and wasn't as sure.

"In this case it wasn't just about money. Edgar had yet to prove himself, and he knew this cattle drive was his best chance. Still, he hated the idea of leaving Evangeline Rose, and with someone named Dirk, of all things. Ken had promised to put in a good word when they returned, but Edgar didn't quite trust her, and so he insisted on meeting his love one last time before they left. So the night before they departed from San Francisco, Ken brought Edgar to Evangeline Rose's window, and—"

"Hold up. Her window?" Claire wrinkled her nose. "Isn't that sort of stalker-y?"

"Yeah, Dad," Patrick chimed in. "That's super creepy."

Their dad laughed. "Maybe your ancestor was a creepy guy."

"Great," Claire muttered. Then she remembered how Mike had come to *her* window, and her face flushed. It hadn't seemed as creepy when he did that, mostly because he was so awkward and earnest and she'd known him forever. He was just *Mike*.

She pictured Mike, and then Justin, who was his opposite in so many ways. Cool and confident instead of awkward. The kind of boy who could fit in anywhere.

Guilt immediately washed over Claire, and she dropped that thought.

"Or maybe," her dad continued, "he met her in her back garden instead."

"Who?" Claire asked, confused.

"Wrong Way Jacobus," Patrick said. "Who else?"

"Oh, yeah." Claire carefully studied the scenery outside, trying to ignore the scarlet cheeks in her reflection in the window.

"He crept in among the rose bushes," her dad continued, "and waited until Ken brought her to see him. As soon as their eyes met, Edgar threw himself to his knees in front of her and proclaimed his undying love."

"Dramatic," Claire said.

"And stupid," Patrick added.

"A fair assessment, on both counts. But in this case ... it was effective."

"Really?" Patrick said.

"Oh, yes. You forget, Edgar may not have had money or fame. But he had one thing in spades, and that was the ole

Jacobus charm." He grinned. "Plus, just like your dad, he was one heck of a handsome guy."

"Ugh, Dad." Claire rolled her eyes.

"Evangeline told Edgar she didn't want to marry Dirk, who viewed her as a prop more than a person, but that she couldn't run away with just anyone. 'Solve one riddle, and I am yours,' she said. 'Tell me, what is my heart's greatest desire?'

"Edgar thought that sounded complicated. 'Er, how about I just go forth and make my fortune to prove myself to you?'

"But Evangeline wisely told him, 'Not all women care about money.'"

"Thanks, Dad." Claire hid her smile with one hand.

"Of course, Edgar didn't know her heart's desire, and so he left her there. But she warned him before he slipped away that she'd be marrying Dirk in a year's time. He had until then to return and solve that riddle, or she'd be lost to him forever."

"So what did he do, Dad?" Patrick whispered.

"He went on that cattle drive, where Ken immediately charmed Johnny into becoming *her* sidekick, leaving Edgar on the outskirts. He knew if things got tense, he'd be the one left behind, and that made him nervous. Still, they had their herd, and they were making great progress, until one rainy, windswept night, when one of the cows cried out in pain. She fell to her knees, and Edgar realized: she was giving birth..."

Edgar labored with her all through the night. Even after a few weeks on the trail, he didn't know much about cows, but he knew a lot about bread, and about working hard in hot, sticky, stressful conditions. And in the deepest, darkest part of night, he finally pulled forth a baby calf.

This calf was pure black, as black as the ocean on a moonless night, except for one tiny spot around her left eye. "I'll name you... Rye," Edgar declared, toweling her off.

The mother cow gave a piteous moan, and Edgar checked her, noticing another pair of hoofs sticking out. "A second calf?"

"Seems like an ill omen," Johnny said. He and Ken had stayed a careful distance away this whole time. "I'd suggest you leave her, and the other calf, too."

"Would I leave a loaf of bread to burn in the oven?" Edgar demanded.

"I'm guessing... maybe?" Johnny said.

"He probably leaves it in the oven a week," Ken said. She'd tried eating a bite of Edgar's baguette at the start of their journey and almost lost a tooth.

Edgar glared at both of them. "The answer is no. No, I would *not* leave a loaf of bread to burn in the oven. Obviously."

"Didn't seem so obvious to me," Johnny muttered, but Edgar ignored him, gritted his teeth, and went back to work.

The second calf was born just as the first faint rays of the sun struck the earth. This calf was a pure, milky white, except for a black ring around his right eye. "I shall name you ... Sourdough."

"That's a terrible name," Johnny said.

"Doesn't matter," Ken cut in. "It's good that they have terrible names, although it would be far better if they had no names at all."

"Why?" Edgar asked. He was completely exhausted, so tired even his bones ached.

Ken flashed her most wicked grin. "Because that way you won't get too attached to them."

Edgar frowned. "Why shouldn't I get attached?" But just at that moment, the mother cow gave another piteous moan ... and died.

"Wait, she *died*?" Claire scowled. "What is this, some kind of Disney story?"

"It's not my fault, honey," her dad said. "I'm just recounting the events as they happened."

"Yeah, right."

"Is this it?" Patrick asked suddenly. "It looks like they're slowing."

Her dad frowned as he slowed down, too, their van bumping along a narrow dirt road. Trees hugged too close on either side, and every few seconds came the awful scrape of a branch gouging the top of their van. Claire felt her teeth rattle, and there was nothing but dust all around as they continued jostling along.

And then finally they stopped in a small clearing. Up ahead, Celeste had already thrown open the doors to her van and leapt out, dancing around with her arms outstretched. "Welcome, welcome," she trilled.

Claire got out of their van and looked around. It just looked like a clearing in the woods next to a pitted dirt road. No bathrooms in sight, no barbecues, no nothing.

Her dad dropped a hand on her shoulder, squeezed. "See?" he said. "Hashtag vanlife."

"Hashtag vanlife," Claire agreed, saying the words easily now.

"Ugh, let's get this over with," Patrick said, stomping away.

Claire and her dad exchanged looks, and then he shrugged. "I guess there's gotta be one in every crowd. The great balance of my life. But, do me a favor, would you? Try to include your brother, at least a little. Okay? I think he's feeling left out."

Claire sighed. "Yes, Dad," she promised.

CHAPTER 24

Claire kept her promise, and so Patrick tagged along as Justin taught her how to climb trees and identify bird tracks and gave her tips for surviving in the wilderness. "I'd be totally fine, you know, if my parents left me out here. I'm a survivor. That's the real reason why I sleep outside the van any chance I get. I like to feel the trees around me, so I can be a part of nature."

"Wow," Claire said.

"A hammock is really the best way to go, because that way you're a part of nature, but you're also a little above it."

"We sleep in hammocks, too," Patrick said.

Justin frowned. "I guess so. But they're not, like, *real* hammocks."

"Why not?" Patrick asked.

"Because you can't hang them from a tree."

Claire hadn't realized there could be fake hammocks. But obviously Justin knew about these things.

"I know about these things," he confirmed. "Real hammocks are great, though. I mean, unless you're scared of bears." He ran a hand back through his thick chestnut-brown hair, tousling it so it fell around his face. "*I'm* not afraid of bears, of course."

"Of course," Patrick muttered, kicking at the dirt. "I'm going to see Dad."

Claire watched her brother stomp away. He seemed so . . . small. For a second she thought about going after him, but then Justin smiled at her, his crooked smile, and staying here suddenly seemed like a much better idea. Patrick would be fine. Besides, she had spent so much time with her brother lately, it was kind of nice getting a break. "Have you seen a bear before?" she asked Justin.

"Oh, yeah." He kicked a rock. "One time a bear was even right over my hammock. I could see its teeth and smell the death on its breath. I thought it was my time, you know?"

Claire nodded, pretending that she did know. "And what happened next?"

"Well, I growled at the bear."

"You growled?"

"Yes. Like this." And he made a sound low in his throat. It sounded a lot like Ronnie's cat choking up a hairball.

Claire giggled, but stopped immediately at the look on Justin's face. Clearly he hadn't meant it to be funny. "Sorry—" she began.

"Oh, Justin!" Celeste called. "We need you, dear heart."

Justin sighed. "Another video, probably." He glanced at Claire, frowning slightly, like he was reevaluating her. Like he'd decided maybe she wasn't the funny, cool, confident girl he'd first thought she was. Her stomach sank. But then he asked, "Want to meet up again when I'm done? We can go do something together."

Claire's heart raced. Do something? Hadn't they *been* doing things? "Um, sure," she said, even though she didn't know what he meant.

He touched her cheek, the tips of his fingers grazing her skin. Claire froze, not even breathing. "See you around, Claire." He dropped his hand, then headed to his van.

Claire stood there for a long time, then went back to her own van, her face still burning in the places Justin had touched her.

The side door of the van was already open. Patrick sat inside at the table, playing around with a toy train he'd gotten at the museum.

Claire leaned her head inside. "You okay?"

Patrick shrugged.

"That's it? I've been your sister your whole life, and that's all the response I get?"

He sighed and looked up at her. "I don't like Justin."

"You...what? Why?"

"Because he's a jerk."

Claire flinched. "How would you know? You haven't even given him a chance. Just because Dad likes spending time with him—"

"That's not it!"

She narrowed her eyes. "You didn't like when Mike came over and helped out with the van, either."

"Mike was just helping to impress you."

Claire's stomach lurched. "What? No."

Patrick snorted. "Dad told him how Edgar impressed Evangeline Rose, and suddenly Mike was all about helping with our van. Because he's, like, in love with you." Patrick grimaced, like that was the grossest thing ever, grosser even than a mouthful of peas.

"H-how do you...I mean, that's ridiculous." Claire's cheeks felt too warm. When had her brother gotten so perceptive? "Whatever."

"Whatever," he mimicked.

"Look, you got mad at me for not trying with this whole hashtag vanlife thing, so here's me trying. I'm doing it. And now *you're* the one being a baby about it."

"I'm not!"

"Oh yeah? You're just sitting in here." She crossed her arms. "You're being *unfun*."

Patrick flinched as if she'd just slapped him.

"Claire?" Justin called.

Claire whirled. "Oh! Hey. Photoshoot already done?"

"Photoshoot," Patrick muttered disgustedly.

"Got it in one." Justin took her hand, just like that. Like they held hands all the time. "I want to show you something."

"What is it?" Patrick asked.

Justin blinked. "Oh. Patrick. I . . . didn't see you in there."

"What do you want to show Claire?" Patrick asked, stone-faced.

Justin winked at Claire. "It's a surprise."

When her dad winked, it was just cheesy. But Justin made it look hot.

"What kind of surprise?" Patrick asked, still staring at Justin like he could laser through him with his eyes.

Justin frowned. "Do you not know the meaning of the word 'surprise'?"

And now Claire frowned. Yeah, Patrick was being a total pest, but Justin didn't have to be rude about it. "He's just curious," she said.

Justin's eyes widened. He studied her, then turned back to her brother. "You know, I'm sorry, Patrick," he said. "I'm not really used to having a little brother. But I consider *you* a brother. I hope you realize that."

Patrick didn't say anything, but his fingers tightened on his toy train.

"I mean, you *are* in my caravan," Justin continued.

"So you think of Claire as a sister, then?"

Claire shot him a look, but he was staring hard at Justin and ignored her.

Justin squeezed Claire's hand. "Sure," he told Patrick. "Why not."

Patrick's eyes narrowed. "Can I come with you and Claire, then?"

"Actually, Patrick," Justin said slowly, "how about you and I go on a little adventure of our own? Would you mind, Claire? I'll show Patrick the place I was going to take you, get his brotherly approval."

"That sounds *fun*," Claire said pointedly.

Patrick sighed. "Fine."

"I'll bring you out there after, okay?" Justin gave Claire's hand one last squeeze, and then he let her go. Her fingers felt cold and clammy where he'd been touching them, and as she watched him walk through the woods with Patrick, she wiped them on her shirt.

Patrick glanced back once, and then he turned around and walked with his shoulders stiff, arms straight, until he disappeared into the trees.

Claire sat inside the van and fiddled with Patrick's toy train, then flipped through his train pamphlet describing all the different routes. She couldn't get her brother's expression out of her mind. Like he'd been looking back at her for help.

Which was silly. Yeah, he might not like Justin, but he'd see that he was wrong. Justin was great. Amazing, even . . .

So why did she feel like she'd just thrown her brother on the tracks?

Claire hesitated a moment longer, and then she got up and headed into the woods to search for them. Just in case.

Claire was lost. Every direction she turned there were trees and then more trees. Sometimes bushes or shrubs. She didn't know the difference, and it didn't matter because she was probably going to die out here. She'd starve, or be eaten by a bear, because she wasn't brave and capable like Justin. She wasn't a survivor. And then she'd never know what the difference was between a bush and a shrub. Somehow that seemed really tragic.

Calm down, Claire, she told herself firmly. She squeezed her hands into fists and counted, listening . . .

A noise up ahead. A human noise. Voices? Crying. *Patrick* crying. Claire hurried in that direction. She thought he might have been saying something, but she couldn't hear it over the thundering of her own heartbeat, over the crunching of the leaves under her feet as she ran.

She burst into a little clearing. A stream cut through the middle of it, burbling into a small pond. Her brother sat curled in a miserable lump next to it, alone.

"Patrick?" Claire said.

He lifted his tear-streaked face toward her, still curled around something.

Claire stepped closer, her mouth dry. "Are you ... okay?"

He didn't say anything, just held his hands to his chest.

"What's wrong?" Claire knelt down in front of him. "Where's Justin?"

"Gone," Patrick said, his mouth twisting. "I hate him."

Claire had never heard her brother say that before. "Why?" she asked carefully.

He lowered his hands. Cupped gently inside them sat a small frog. "He forced it to eat a rock." Patrick's voice caught. Tears streamed down his face. "He forced it to, and I couldn't stop him, and he laughed. And I don't know what to do now. I d-don't know how to h-help it." He sobbed, his whole body shaking.

Claire felt numb. Gently, she reached forward and took the small frog from Patrick. It was alive, quivering in her hands. Maybe Justin made up a story? Something to scare Patrick? Which was terrible enough, but she couldn't imagine he'd—

She felt something in the frog's stomach. Small and hard and immovable. Claire swayed, as around her the clearing seemed to erupt with the song of a hundred frogs, all croaking, mournful. She sat on the ground and put an arm around Patrick's shoulders, and felt like she'd swallowed a rock, too.

"I'm sorry," she whispered, both to the frog and to her brother. "I'm sorry." She met her brother's eyes. "But I promise, somehow I will make this right."

CHAPTER 25

Claire and Patrick managed to find their way out of the woods, although Claire felt like she was bringing half of it with her, leaves and twigs tangled in her hair, and dirt streaked down her face. She'd never wanted a shower so badly in her life.

Or maybe it was just the sight of Justin up ahead that made her long to dunk herself under scalding hot water.

She pictured her brother crying while this boy laughed, and her heart turned to stone. How had she ever thought he was handsome?

Patrick had stopped crying, but he kept the frog cuddled against his chest as he walked, and Claire noticed it wasn't moving. Once in a while it would make a noise like it was trying to croak, but couldn't.

Why would Justin do something so unnecessarily cruel?

"Go find Dad," Claire whispered to her brother. "He might know how to help the frog."

Patrick stopped walking. "Do you really think Dad might be able to help him?"

No, was the honest answer. But instead she said, "If anyone would know, he would," and that wasn't a lie. Not really.

He still didn't move. "What are you going to do?"

"I'm going to talk to Justin."

Justin was walking barefoot across a long cord his parents had stretched between two trees. They called it slacklining. Claire had tried it a few times, but she kept stumbling off. The last time, Justin had laughed and held one of her hands, guiding her along. "Look at you! A natural," he'd said, followed by that crooked smile, and Claire had thought—

It didn't matter what she'd thought. Even though that was only yesterday, it felt like a whole different time in her life. A time Before, when she'd thought she was in love with Justin, and then there was Now, when she knew better. Even if she could still remember the twist in her stomach when he looked at her. And maybe there was an explanation, some . . . misunderstanding. Maybe he hadn't meant to make the frog eat a rock. Or maybe . . .

Patrick was staring at her, his lower lip jutting.

"What?" Claire asked.

"Why do you want to talk to Justin?"

"To see what he has to say."

That lower lip quivered. "You don't believe me, do you? He said you wouldn't. He said you'd listen to him, and—"

"Patrick." Claire put both her hands on his shoulders and leaned forward until her face was only inches from his. "I believe you."

"Promise?" His eyes searched her face. So intense. Funny how he always looked so much like their dad, except in these quiet moments.

She gave his shoulders one last gentle squeeze. "I promise," she said, and then she let him go.

She curled her hands into tight fists as she walked toward Justin, mentally counting, and then relaxed her hands. But as her fingers straightened, she still didn't know what she was going to do, just that she would have to do *something*. "Hey, Justin."

He slipped off the line, stumbling a few steps before he caught himself. "Hey, Claire." His brow furrowed. "You know, it's not safe to sneak up on someone on a slackline. I know you don't really know the etiquette, so I won't blame you, but—"

"Patrick told me about the frog and the rock." Claire didn't care about etiquette or slacklining or Justin and his "you knows."

"Ah." Justin ran a hand through his hair. He did that so often, it was actually kind of annoying.

"Is it true?"

"Is what true?"

Claire took a deep breath, let it out. Her fingers ached. "Did you make a frog eat a rock?"

He sighed, looking disappointed. "You know, you're the first girl I ever felt really understood me. Like, we have this connection. Not everyone gets vanlife, or being in nature, but *you* do. You *get* me. Or, I thought you did." He shook his head, his hair falling into his eyes.

For one traitorous second, she was flattered. But she'd heard enough stories in her life to recognize when someone was spinning a tale.

Spinning a tale. And now, finally, she knew what to do.

"*You know*," Claire said, "that's really not an answer."

Justin pushed his hair back and finally looked at her straight. "I was just trying to get your brother to back off a little, okay?" he said, annoyed. "He's always lurking, and I want to spend time with *you*." He caught her hands, and she let him. Her fingers felt icy cold, numb, like they belonged to someone else. "Besides, it's just a frog."

Claire pictured her brother by that pond, crying, helpless as Justin tortured that frog right in front of him. The numbness spread, washing over her and filling her vision with spots. "Just a frog," she repeated. Her own voice sounded hollow in her ears, like it belonged to someone else.

"That's right." Justin's grin was back in full force. "There are literally hundreds by that pond. It's ridiculous. And that croaking sound..." He shuddered. "It's gross. I mean, I *love* nature, you know. But I never really liked frogs."

Claire blinked, and the numbness slid from her like a blanket, the world snapping into a focus so sharp, it was almost blinding. "I heard a strange fact about frogs once." The words seemed to slide off her tongue as she casually pulled her hands free of Justin's. "You know how a group of crows is called a murder?"

"Obviously."

"Well, I bet you didn't know that a group of frogs is called a suffocation."

"What? That's stupid."

"A suffocation of frogs," Claire said. "And it's not so stupid when you find out why they got that name."

Justin hesitated. But Claire realized she was a better story spinner than he was, and in the end he couldn't stop himself from asking, "How did they get that name?"

Hook, line, and sucker.

Claire smiled. "Ah, that's an interesting story."

Long ago, back before cities and roads and vans, jungles claimed most of this land, and the lions claimed the jungles. And far below the canopy, unnoticed by the lions, lived the humble frogs, who preferred it that way. If no one saw them, no one hunted them. It was only when the sun went down that they would come out to sing to the moon and its beauty, the way it reflected in silvery ripples on the surface of their beloved pond, and to taste the night that surrounded them.

Back then, frogs didn't croak. Instead, they hummed melodies. Each frog had a different note, so when a family of them got together, they harmonized. And while there wasn't a name for a group of frogs yet, if there had been, it would have been a song of frogs.

As time passed, humans took over the rule of the jungle from the lions. The frogs watched them come with interest, but no real fear. After all, they were just frogs. Who would bother with them? And so during the day, they observed the humans with their axes and ploughs, chiseling away at the edges of the forest, and at night they continued to enjoy the cool waters of their favorite pond.

But then one day, one of the humans, a lowly boy with a smile as crooked as his heart, noticed the song of the frogs. Intrigued, he followed the sound to their pond. He was tall and clever, with sharp eyes and quick hands, and he liked to catch the frogs, snatching them from their lily pads faster than a frog's tongue snatches a fly from the air. He'd hang on to them for a little while, and then he'd let them go.

The frogs weren't sure what to do about this boy.

He isn't hurting us, one family hummed.

Yet, came the reply.

Yet.

Yet.

The boy grew bolder. He could now snatch whole families at a time, and he'd poke them, prod them, try to get them to sing different notes. Still, as the morning light brushed its tendrils against the surface of the water, he would let them go and return to his home.

Days passed like this, then weeks. Frogs don't have a good sense of time, but as the boy kept devising new things to do to them, fear rose up in their throats, changing their songs. He would trap them in cages and submerge them slowly underwater. Put them in pots with walls too high for them to climb, and leave them out baking in the sun.

The frogs were scared and restless. Especially the Mossofrogs. These were a family of the largest frogs. They moved slower, and all too often they were the ones caught by the boy. *We need to do something,* they sang. *We need to fight back, to protect ourselves.*

We are frogs, hummed the other families. *We do not fight. We sing.*

As long as we still have our songs, the Mossofrogs reluctantly agreed. *But what if we lose them?*

Then we fight, the other frogs agreed.

Then, we fight.

And then one day...the boy caught the head of the Mossofrog family, a giant bull of a frog, so large he filled both of the boy's hands.

The boy was fascinated by how ugly this frog was. Where the boy's skin was smooth and lovely, this frog's skin was bumpy, rough, and covered in warts. And when the boy looked into the frog's large black eyes, he saw reflected back the color of his own heart.

Furious at this glimpse of the truth, the boy slowly choked the frog, who called out for help. The frog's lovely, melodic song became rougher, trapped, until nothing but a loud croak emerged.

And in the trees, under logs, below lily pads, the other frogs watched as the boy laughed his cruel, mocking laugh. As the boy took the song from this defenseless frog, forever.

After he was done, the boy dropped the frog and went back to his home.

He liked to sleep out under the open sky, because he enjoyed feeling the trees around him, even though the trees were always whispering, *You don't belong here. You don't belong.* But he never bothered to actually listen to the trees. He wanted to be a part of nature, but also a little above it, so he shut his ears to anything but his own noisy thoughts.

Which is too bad, because on this night, as the boy made his bed in the forest, the trees had another message for him: *They are coming.* The boy ignored the rustling of the leaves, the creaking of the branches. He didn't listen to the way the wind shifted, or how the forest grew still. And he definitely didn't hear the song of a thousand silent frogs, all creeping up to him, closer, closer...

"Stop it!" Justin took a step back, his face twisted into an ugly mask. "I know what you're doing. You're making all this up!"

Claire blinked. For a second she'd been in that forest, she'd been one of the frogs creeping silently toward her unsuspecting prey. She could almost taste the night around her, feel the blades of grass beneath her webbed feet. Was *this* why her dad told troll stories? Because *he* enjoyed them? Because he liked imagining another world running below theirs?

"Don't you want to know how the story ends?" she asked. "I haven't gotten to the best part yet."

"I don't care."

"You see, while he was sleeping, the frogs covered the boy, every inch of him. And when he woke and tried to scream—"

"I said *stop!*" Justin took another step back, his eyes wide and fearful. This boy who claimed he was so brave he could face down bears, scared of a story about frogs.

Claire almost felt bad, but then she pictured that poor frog, helpless in Justin's hand, the way it must have felt when he shoved that rock down its throat. Could it still breathe? Did it know it would die soon? "Don't worry," she whispered. "The frogs paid a price for their actions."

Justin stopped backing away from her. "Oh yeah? Did the boy stomp them all to death?"

Claire shook her head. She felt strangely calm, as if all her anger had been channeled out into this story. "They lost the ability to sing, and that's why they croak now instead. But sometimes, if you get enough of them together, it still almost sounds like they're singing. If you listen closely enough. Which is good, because as long as they still have their songs, they're content to be frogs. But if one of them loses that song..."

Justin's eyes narrowed, becoming slits in his red, puffy face. "What?" he sneered. "They attack?"

Claire shrugged.

Justin leaned away from her, but he needed to have the whole story before he could go. "What happened to the boy in the story?"

Claire paused. "Like I said before, there's a reason they're now called a *suffocation* of frogs."

Justin's mouth fell open, and he scrambled away from her. "You're sick, you know that? You're a freak, just like your brother. Just like your dad!" He turned and ran, disappearing inside his van.

Claire waited for the anger to come roaring back, but it didn't. Maybe it was because his words didn't matter. She'd forget them long before *he'd* forget *her* words. "Just try sleeping outside in your stupid hammock now," she whispered. He'd hear the frogs in the night, and he'd lie awake and picture them creeping toward him. And it would serve him right.

She turned. Patrick stood behind her, half-hidden in the trees. "That," he said, "was *awesome!*"

"As good as one of Dad's stories?"

"Better! Seriously, I think I'm more scared of frogs now than I ever was of trolls."

Claire laughed, and it only hitched a little. "Don't tell Dad that. The last thing we need is for him to tell us more troll stories." She bit her lip. Patrick's hands were empty. "How's the frog?"

He looked away from her. "Dad ... he said he'd be able to remove the rock if he took it to the pond. But he didn't want me to watch. Because it'll be messy." *Because he's lying,* Claire realized. Her dad was making up a frog story, too, and

Patrick knew it. Patrick knew the truth, but could pretend to believe the story instead, if he wanted.

It was like her dad was giving him a choice.

Claire swallowed the sudden lump in her throat. "We should probably pack up our stuff," she managed, eyeing Justin's van. The side door had just opened, and Celeste poked her head out, looking murderous. "I have a feeling we're not going to be super popular around here anymore."

CHAPTER 26

Claire watched her dad's neck muscles bunch as he drove. His jaw kept twitching, too. And his knuckles were white on the steering wheel. He was really angry. Really, really angry. Even without those telltale physical signs, she'd know that; she could feel the anger radiating off him like waves in a storm.

This was the first time she and Patrick had argued—silently—over who got to sit on the cooler in back. Claire had won, for once. And even though she still didn't trust her dad's seatbelt, she knew she felt safer perched on this cooler than Patrick felt sitting up front.

"So," their dad said finally. They'd been driving for almost an hour in complete silence. Not even music. Nothing. "You thought it would be funny to scare some poor kid with some kind of, of *horror* story."

"Oh, real nice, coming from you," Claire huffed. "Mister 'trolls kidnap children in the night.'"

Her dad had the grace to flinch, but a second later, his face was as stern as before. "That's because *my* kids are Jacobuses. I knew they could handle it."

"Justin claimed he was very brave," Claire said.

"You know as well as I do that only someone who is *pretending* to be brave would be so loud about it. Truly brave people don't go around proclaiming it."

"Well, Justin deserved that story," Patrick said darkly.

"That's right," Claire said. "Really, he's just lucky his parents kicked us out of camp before Patrick and I could implement phase two."

"Phase two?" their dad asked. Claire could see him struggling to hold on to his anger, but in the end, he was a sucker for a story, too, and he couldn't stop himself from asking, "What was phase two?"

"We were going to collect a bucketful of frogs and dump them into Justin's hammock while he was sleeping."

Their dad chuckled. And then his chuckle turned into a laugh, and then a bellow, until finally he had to pull over to the side of the road, he was laughing so hard. Eventually, he wiped his streaming eyes and shook his head. "Ah, kiddos, I'm sorry. I'm sure if you were both united in such an... *unusual* plan, then Justin must have done something, and I didn't even notice. I was too busy vanlifing it up." He sighed. "Want to tell me about it?"

Patrick shrugged.

"Does it have something to do with the frog I rescued? The one you just happened to find?"

Patrick shrugged again, and then the words tumbled out, about Justin and the pond and Claire's story. When he was done, their dad nodded once, slowly, like he was making a decision.

"Well," he said. "I can see I've certainly rubbed off on you, Claire." He rubbed his jaw uneasily, and then broke into a grin. "Not quite sure how I feel about that, honestly."

"Me neither," Claire admitted.

"I bet Justin practices smiling in a mirror," Patrick said. "No one smiles like that unless it's on purpose."

Claire snorted. "You're probably right. And his parents? *Celeste?* Like that was her real name. And P-Sign? You don't see me going around calling myself C-Sign, do you? So ridiculous."

"C-Sign?" Her dad raised his eyebrows. "Oh. You thought he meant . . ." He chuckled, shook his head. "He meant Peace Sign, honey. It was a play on the first letter of his name, and yeah, a little ridiculous, but"—he shrugged—"van people."

"Whoa, no way," Patrick breathed.

"What?" Claire glanced at her brother. His eyes were wide, mouth open like he'd just figured out the secret of the universe.

"I thought he meant...um"—Patrick dropped his voice—
"*pee* sign," he explained. "Like, you know, in a toilet?"

Claire got it. "Pee sign," she said, exchanging a look
with her dad. And then they were laughing again, and Claire
thought she might die because she couldn't breathe. "Pee-
sign," she choked.

"This whole time," Patrick giggled. "This whole time,
whenever someone called him, I thought, I thought," he
gasped, took a deep breath, "I thought there must be some
wacky story behind that name."

And they all roared with laughter until the walls of the
van shook with it. It filled every last inch of space, and as
Claire finally caught her breath, she realized that for the first
time since they'd left their house behind, she felt like she'd
finally come home.

"You kids." Their dad chuckled. "And you know, I
shouldn't have made that *van people* comment. *We're* van
people, after all."

"And I liked all the other van people we've met," Patrick
said.

"I suppose it's like any group, a mixture of good and
bad." He restarted the van, then headed back on the road.
"Did you know that a group of frogs used to be called a har-
mony?"

"Really?" Claire said.

"Really. So you're not that far off."

"I thought I'd made that completely up."

"Interesting how that works, huh?" He glanced in the rearview mirror, changing lanes.

"What's a group of frogs called now, Dad?" Patrick asked.

"An army."

"A suffocation of frogs sounds a lot cooler," Patrick decided. "I'm going to call it that from now on."

"Me, too," his dad agreed. "You remember your grandfather's motto?"

"Never let the facts get in the way of a good story," Patrick recited.

"Exactly. If I teach you nothing else in this life, I hope I've at least taught you that."

They drove in silence for a little while as the sun began drifting down below the trees.

"How do you all feel about Utah?" he asked suddenly.

"Utah?" Claire said.

Patrick shrugged. "I'm fine with Utah."

"Doesn't Aunt Jan live in Salt Lake City?" Claire asked.

Silence thickened inside the van. "Yes," her dad said finally. "I was thinking that maybe we'd pay her a visit."

"Really?" Claire asked.

"I thought it might be nice to reconnect." Her dad tapped the steering wheel. Claire was beginning to realize that it was more a nervous gesture than a possessive one.

Their aunt used to come over for Thanksgiving, and sometimes she'd stay through Christmas. And then one year she just...stopped. She still sent birthday cards with cash in them, and when Claire broke her wrist, her aunt had sent flowers. Which was nice, because Claire had never been sent flowers before.

Her aunt would be practically a stranger now. Still, Claire couldn't help but feel a surge of excitement, because even if her aunt didn't have flowers for her this time, she'd definitely have indoor plumbing. But..."Why?" she asked her dad.

He shrugged. "Sibling relationships, and family, and all that."

"All that," Patrick said wisely. "But, I thought she was cursed by a witch?"

"Yes, well. Maybe she's better now. I'll give her a call tomorrow and make sure it's okay if we swing by. We wouldn't be arriving for another day or two anyhow." He pursed his lips. "Maybe don't mention that whole curse thing if we go there. She's probably pretty sensitive about it."

"Where are we going tonight?" Patrick asked.

"There's a truck stop a couple hours down the road. We could sleep in their parking lot."

"Doesn't that just sound the funnest," Claire sighed.

"I think they have showers."

"Deal," Claire said immediately.

"I thought that might be an easy sell."

They drove in silence a little farther, the familiar rumble of the diesel engine rattling below their feet. They'd been camping for less than a week, but Claire was surprised to realize that she'd actually missed being on the road.

"Are you two burned out on stories?" her dad asked. "Or did you want to hear the next part of Wrong Way's tale? This time it's about the baby calves."

It almost felt like an apology. "We'd love to hear it, Dad," Claire said. Patrick nodded.

Her dad smiled and began his story.

CHAPTER 27

Edgar grew to love Rye and Sourdough. It was the first time in his life that anyone had ever depended on him, and it made him feel equal parts terrified and like he was finally in the right place at the right time, like his talents had somehow lined up. He might not be good at baking bread or discovering the secrets of a woman's heart's desire, but he sure was good at caring for those baby cows.

When they made it out to Kansas City, in Kansas, not Missouri, Johnny pulled him aside. "Look, Edgar, Kennedy made some inquiries, and...those calves are worth a lot of money."

"They are?"

"Oh, yes." Johnny rubbed his hands together. "Apparently twin calves of black and white will fetch you a fortune out here. As much as the rest of the herd combined."

His eyes gleamed like brand-new pennies. "We are going to be rich, my friend!"

"Really?" Edgar laid a hand on Rye's soft black head, and his other hand on Sourdough's wet pink nose.

"I know, it's quite surprising. Good thing we didn't leave them to die after all, eh?" Johnny clapped Edgar on the back.

Edgar could feel his calves staring up at him with their big cow eyes, and his stomach sank. How could he sell them? "Who would buy them?"

"Oh, someone looking for a good set of leathers, no doubt." Johnny shrugged like he didn't care. Because he didn't.

But Edgar cared. Edgar cared a lot. He looked into the eyes of his two young charges. They looked back at him, all innocent and trusting. Sourdough wiped his nose on Edgar's pants. Rye licked his hand. "The way I see it," Edgar said slowly, turning back to Johnny, "I delivered these calves myself. So they belong to me."

Johnny frowned. "What are you saying? That you don't plan to split the profits?"

"I'm saying that I don't plan to get the profits. I'm not selling them."

Johnny's frown turned into a scowl. "You can't do that, Edgar. We did this cattle drive together, you and me and Ken. All the long, hot days baking in the sun and covered in horse hair. All the sleepless, chilly nights. The rain and the mud and the constant threat of predators. We faced all that together then. We split it all together now."

Edgar knew, then, that he would be severing his friendship with Johnny forever. His only friend in the States. But those calves looked to him for protection, and that was worth more than any money. More, even, than the hand of the beautiful Evangeline Rose. Edgar made up his mind that he would give up his chance at a fortune, if it meant keeping his calves safe. "You and Ken can split my share of the rest of the cattle drive," he said. "And I'll just take these calves."

"That's not a fair deal, and you know it." Johnny spat.

Edgar looked at him a long, long time. "It's the only deal I'm willing to make," he said. "Take it or leave it. Because friend or no, I will fight you on this."

"Friend? We ain't friends," Johnny said. "Not anymore." He looked back over his shoulder, at where Ken was talking to the man who'd hired them. "But on account of our past friendship, I'm going to give you a head start. You understand me, Edgar?" He looked Edgar close in the eye. "Ken'll kill you herself with the knives she has hidden in her long, long hair. She'll kill you and your little cows. So you'd better run, and run fast. Take both horses. You'll need to rotate out if you're gonna have a chance. And when we catch up with you, I'm gonna claim you stole them, you hear me?"

"I hear you loud and clear. And . . . I'm sorry things had to end this way."

"Me too, Edgar. Me, too." Johnny hesitated, and then he clapped Edgar on the back again. "I don't want to have to kill you."

"I don't want that, either." And even though Edgar felt like his bones were made of lead, he got Rye, Sourdough, and both horses ready to go.

"Why do you do this?" Johnny asked suddenly.

"Do what?"

"Everything you do, you do it wrong. No matter which way is the easy way, it's like you are compelled to do the opposite."

Edgar shrugged. "What can I say? Easy is boring." He tipped his hat to his former friend and disappeared into the dust of the trail.

But one thing bothered him, as he raced through that day and into the night. Johnny hadn't said *if we catch up with you*, but rather *when*. And it was that *when* that spurred Edgar on long after he thought he might collapse. He stopped only when Rye or Sourdough needed a break, but otherwise, he kept moving.

On the third day, he came across a sign with his face and the faces of Rye and Sourdough. WANTED, the sign read. DEAD OR ALIVE. EDGAR "WRONG WAY" JACOBUS, FOR THE CRIME OF CATTLE RUSTLING.

"You see that, Rye?" Edgar, now Wrong Way, said. "That's how a person earns a name."

"Moo," Rye agreed.

"I knew you'd understand." Wrong Way patted his calf on the head, then spared an extra pat for Sourdough. "Can't have you feeling left out, now can we?"

Something about seeing his face in print like that, his face with a new name, made Wrong Way understand what it was that Evangeline's heart desired. He'd traveled under the baking sun, and he'd traveled under the wide blue sky. He'd experienced thunderstorms, and lightning, and torrential rain, as well as wind that whipped around so fast it stole three of his best hats. He'd been hungry, and tired, and thirsty.

But out there on the open road was the first time Edgar had ever felt alive, truly and completely. It was as if he'd gone into this country one person, and by journeying all those miles, he'd become someone else. And along the way, he'd realized something.

There was nothing wrong with the bread he used to bake for his uncle. It was perfectly good, as long as you didn't try to eat it. Just like there was nothing wrong with a woman like Evangeline Rose, unless you tried to force her into a boring life married to a man like Dirk. That would never be a fit for someone with her wild heart. But give her a chance at a new life, and she could earn herself a new name, too.

She could reinvent herself however she wanted.

But once again, Edgar was going about everything the wrong way. Only this time, there'd be no fixing it.

* * *

"Wait, what do you mean, no fixing it?" Patrick demanded. "Doesn't Edgar rescue Evangeline Rose from Dirk?"

"Did she need rescuing?" their dad asked.

"Well, yeah."

"Don't you think she could have left Dirk herself, if she'd really wanted to? Remember, this is the woman who fought off Johnny's brother with a bag. She was strong enough to do anything, go anywhere, if she truly wanted to."

Patrick frowned. "But . . . if she's our great-great-great-grandmother, she has to marry Edgar. He has to get there in time to stop the wedding."

"*Is* she our great-great-great-grandmother?" Claire asked. She couldn't remember if her dad had ever actually confirmed that.

"Hmm, good question," he said.

"Noncommittal answer," Claire shot back.

He grinned. "You're getting better with your words all the time. How about this for an answer: stories don't always end the way we'd hope."

Patrick's frown deepened, and he looked out the window.

"But, in this case, since I can see the lights of the truck stop ahead, I'll skip a little and tell you that Edgar does manage to stop the wedding. Just like every movie ever made, he arrives in town just as the church bells are ringing, sprints down that aisle in the nick of time, tells Evangeline he has the answer, defeats Dirk in a vicious bread-versus-pistol duel, and then carries Evangeline away. It was only afterward that he realized his mistake, and by then it was too late."

Their dad pulled into the truck stop parking lot and found a spot near the back, then shut off the engine. "But for better or worse," he concluded, "Edgar whisked Evangeline Rose away to the land of lakes, to Michigan, and there us Jacobuses have been ever since." He opened his door and hopped out. "Grab your toothbrushes, kids. It's time to get ready for bed, yeah?" He closed the door behind him.

"But . . . what was it Evangeline really wanted, then?" Patrick asked.

"I don't know," Claire said. "And it sounds like maybe Dad doesn't, either." She thought about her dad's story as she followed her brother out of the van. Now that she'd told her own story, she knew it wasn't really a lie. She'd made everything up, but there had been a meaning to it, a deeper truth.

Maybe her dad's stories worked the same way. Maybe he was trying to tell them something that he'd never be able to explain any other way.

CHAPTER 28

W ow, look at all those mountains." Patrick pressed his nose against the window as they made their way into Salt Lake City.

"It feels like we're cupped inside them, like they're a giant hand," Claire said.

"That's awfully romantic of you, Claire-bear." Her dad's back was unnaturally straight, and he kept making his thinking face, puckering his lips, his forehead creasing.

"Are you nervous?" Claire asked.

"Nervous? Me? Ha!"

"Definitely nervous," Patrick said.

"Did Aunt Jan say we could visit?" Claire asked.

"Hmm? Oh, yes. Of course."

"So you talked to her?"

"Of course," he said again, but distractedly.

Claire imagined the feeling of a hot shower and plenty of soap. And...a bed. "Do you think we could stay in her house?"

"What?"

"I mean, I love the van—"

"You do?" Patrick gaped. "Did you really just say that? Dad, did you hear what she said?"

"I heard, I heard."

"I..." Claire paused. "I mean..." Why had she said that? But she realized it wasn't a lie. Somewhere along the way, the van had begun feeling almost like...home. "I still don't like the name."

"Van-Helsing? What's not to like?" Patrick grinned.

"Anyhow," Claire said, "my point is, the van is okay, I guess—"

Patrick's grin stretched wider—that irritating, irritating grin.

"—but I'd love to sleep in something that isn't a hammock for a night," she finished.

Her dad nodded. "Jan has a large house. I'm sure she'll be delighted to have you stay inside it. But first...did you know Salt Lake City has a phenomenal natural history museum?"

"Dad," Claire and Patrick both groaned.

"Kids," he mimicked. "It's too early for dinner. What do you say we head over and just kill a few hours. Eh?"

Patrick twisted around in the front seat. "What do you think?" he asked Claire.

"I think we should make Dad get us ice cream first," Claire decided.

"Ooh, good point. I also read there's a train station here," Patrick said. "Maybe we can go look at it?"

"Is there?" Claire asked.

"Yeah. The California Zephyr goes right through Salt Lake City."

"The California Zephyr?"

"It's the second-longest route on Amtrak, from San Francisco all the way to Chicago. *And* it's got two stories."

"That's, um, amazing." Claire didn't get Patrick's fascination with trains. They just seemed like airplanes that took forever to get to their destinations. "But even more amazing, I've heard there are bison out here."

"Like, giant woolly bison?" Patrick asked.

"As opposed to the small hairless ones? Yes."

Their dad laughed. "Okay, okay, we'll get ice cream first, and we'll check out the bison tomorrow, okay? Best place to see them is in a place called Antelope Island, but it's a bit of a drive and I think we should save it for an all-day trip tomorrow. We can even camp out there overnight, if you'd like."

"Is it near the Salt Lake?" Claire asked. She'd always wanted to see that. Ronnie told her it was so salty, you could float a rock right on its surface. Claire was pretty sure that was a lie, but she wanted to test it out, just in case.

"We can visit the Salt Lake there, yes. But first, as promised..." He pulled up in front of an outdoor ice cream stand.

"And then the train station?" Patrick asked.

"Well, technically my sister doesn't live too far from the station, so I guess we could swing by. But it's not a big station, and I think it's only open at night. You might be disappointed."

Patrick shrugged.

"It's not an especially great part of town, either," their dad added.

"Does that mean Aunt Jan doesn't live in a great part of town?" Claire asked.

"She's in one of those fancy gated communities, the kind with a guard who has to let you in and everything." His mouth twisted. "So it doesn't really matter what part of town she's in, does it?"

"Wow," Patrick said. "Is she rich?"

Their dad's face twitched. "Depends who you compare her to."

"Compared to us?"

He shook his head. "No one is as rich as us. After all, we've got Van-Helsing, and we're about to get some truly spectacular ice cream." He glanced at Claire. "Notice I didn't combine any words there. Just used one. Spectacular."

"I noticed, Dad. You're getting better."

"That's just because I couldn't figure out how to combine it with amazing." He got out of the van.

"Spectazing?" Patrick suggested, hopping out after him.

"Amazetacular?" their dad tried.

Claire sighed and closed the sliding door behind her. "I take it all back."

He laughed. "Come along, my children. No matter what word we choose, know that here you will get everything your little hearts desire. As long as that thing is soft serve with extra sprinkles."

Claire never saw her dad as excited as he was the moment they stepped inside the natural history museum and up the steps to the lobby. "You kiddos are going to love it here!" He spread his arms wide and spun in a slow circle. "And you hear that? Music!" He did a little shimmy, tapping his feet on the marble floor.

"Dad," Claire hissed. There weren't very many people around, but still.

"What's the matter, Claire-bear? Embarrassed?" His smile was in full force. "How about...now?" He curled all his fingers and stuck out his thumbs. "You embarrassed that your old man is...all thumbs?"

Patrick laughed maniacally.

"Dad, no," Claire moaned, hiding her face. She knew what came next. And sure enough, her dad started doing the thumb dance, his body swaying back and forth, right there in the middle of the museum lobby.

"Stop, Dad. Please," Claire begged.

"The thumb leads and the body follows," he said, moving his shoulders now, really getting into it.

"Excuse me, sir?" a museum attendant called. She was tall, Claire noticed, and pretty, with straight black hair that fell to her shoulders and pink-rimmed glasses.

Her dad stopped dancing, but didn't look at all ashamed of himself. "Oh, was I being disruptive? Sorry, I was just trying to embarrass my daughter."

"And succeeding," Claire muttered.

The woman laughed. "You weren't being disruptive. I appreciate your energy. I just wanted to let you know that the museum is closing early today."

Now he looked properly horrified. "What do you mean, closing early? How early?"

"Like, in twenty minutes early."

"But...but why?"

"Staff party. One of our children's guides is retiring today. It's too bad, because I can tell you would have liked him; he has a pretty mean thumb dance, too."

"Of all the days." He ran a hand across his chin. "So...we can't look around, then?"

She shook her head.

"Do you have any idea what it took to convince my kids to come here? I had to bankrupt myself in ice cream."

"I really am sorry. Feel free to look around the lobby. We do have some exhibits out here, and there's always the gift store. Although you might want to avoid that, considering you're already bankrupt." She winked.

Claire's dad put a hand to his heart, his classic "you wound me" pose, and the attendant giggled.

Claire's mouth fell open. Was her dad...flirting? Eww! "Come on, Patrick," she whispered. "We do not need to see this."

"See what?" he asked, but he let her herd him over to a glass display case that reached all the way up to the very high ceiling. They looked at the skeletons and pottery before wandering over to the giant map in the middle of the room. It listed all the national parks of the United States.

"We should try to visit all of them someday," Claire said.

"Maybe after California."

Claire frowned. "California?"

Patrick shifted uncomfortably. "I was thinking...we'll probably head there next. Right?"

She studied her brother. "You know, Dad hasn't said anything about going there."

Patrick shrugged, and didn't meet her eyes. Did he know something?

Tell him. The words struck Claire so suddenly, she felt like someone must have whispered them in her ear. She glanced behind her. Her dad was filling out some sort of paperwork, still chatting with the worker. For all Claire knew, he was leaving his phone number. She turned back. Patrick was watching her, blue eyes wide.

He didn't remember their mother at all. To him, she was just a character in another story, sometimes a spy, sometimes a princess. Sometimes a woman like Evangeline Rose. He had no idea why she left, and honestly, neither did Claire. And for once, Claire didn't even care, not anymore. All that mattered was that her mom *had* left; she'd left and she wasn't coming back. And Patrick needed to understand that, so he'd stop searching for some kind of fairy-tale ending to this particular tale.

Stories don't always end the way we'd hope.

Claire thought of those divorce papers, that box checked so firmly. No child custody sought. Patrick deserved to know.

"Do you trust me?" she asked him.

"Yes," he said immediately.

"So, you'd tell me if you had a secret, right?"

To her surprise, Patrick's face turned bright red, and he looked away.

"*Do* you have a secret?" she demanded, forgetting that she was leading up to her own.

"Do you . . . do you promise not to be mad?"

"How can I promise that until you tell me what it is?"

"If you don't promise, then I'll never tell you what it is."

"Well that's . . . not really fair."

"It's the only deal I'm willing to make," Patrick quoted, grinning broadly. "Take it or leave it."

"Fine." Claire shook her head. "What is it?"

"Remember when you caught me going through your things? You know, back home?"

"Which time?" Claire asked dryly.

Patrick brushed that off. "I found the address you wrote down. The one in California. You know . . . for Mom."

Claire froze. She'd forgotten she'd written it down. After Ronnie had found Catherine online, Claire had jotted down her mother's name and address on a piece of paper and stuffed it in a drawer, then did her best to forget about it. She didn't plan to look her up or anything. She just liked holding on to something she knew was true. "Look, Patrick—"

"Ready to roll, kiddos?" Their dad dropped a hand on each of their shoulders.

Claire jumped. "We're leaving now?"

"Yeppers."

She sighed. "Dad, add that to your list."

"You have a list?" The museum attendant came up next to them.

"This is Audrey," their dad said. "Audrey, this is my delightful daughter, Claire, my charming son, Patrick, and yes, I have a list of words I am not allowed to say under any circumstances. This list now apparently includes 'yeppers.'"

"My daughter made me a list, too." Audrey looked Claire over. "Let me guess ... thirteen?"

"Twelve," Claire said.

Audrey nodded. "You're mature for your age, aren't you? I can tell."

Claire stood up a little taller. "Thank you."

"Well, we'd better head out. Audrey, it truly was a pleasure." Her dad did that embarrassing thing where he wrapped both of his hands around the other person's hand, and then shook. Ugh. Why couldn't he shake hands like a normal adult? But Audrey seemed to like it, because she smiled again.

"I'll let you know if anything opens up," she said, waving as they headed toward the door.

"Opens up?" Claire asked her dad.

"Eh," he said. "Don't worry about it."

Claire frowned, suddenly *very* worried about it. Whatever *it* was. But before she could argue more, her dad was pointing and saying, "Would you look at that view!" and Claire couldn't help but look.

One full wall of the lobby was made of glass, giving her a clear view of the mountains nearby. They were golden brown against the bright blue of the late-afternoon sky, standing up like a dramatic wall. She imagined climbing up those mountains, exploring the trails that had to be woven through them. "I'm sorry we didn't come out here and visit Aunt Jan before this," she said.

Her dad winced. "Yeah," he said quietly. "I guess I am, too. Although . . . let's wait and see what our reception is like, eh?"

"She *does* know we're coming, right, Dad?"

"Well . . . I got a new phone before we left, and I never saved her number into it. So . . . it'll be a surprise." He grinned. "Won't *that* be an exciting adventure?"

CHAPTER 29

Claire couldn't remember ever having a more awkward dinner. Even at Julian's house. He might have offered her and her eight-year-old brother a beer, but at least he talked. Aunt Jan hadn't said more than a dozen words since she'd first welcomed them inside her surprisingly large house. Apparently she'd known they were coming only when the guard at the gate phoned her for permission to let them pass.

At least the food was good: pad Thai, brown rice, and some sort of spicy green curry. It was a nice change from peanut butter and jelly sandwiches and the occasional diner meal.

"You're an excellent cook," Claire said.

"I'm not," her aunt said flatly. She looked almost exactly the way Claire remembered: short, with hair dyed red from a bottle, wearing a T-shirt and jeans like she was a teenager. Except in Claire's memories, her aunt was smiling.

Not today. Today, she looked like her lips had been nailed to a Popsicle stick.

Claire glanced at her dad. He stabbed morosely at his noodles with a fork; Thai food was not his favorite. Patrick ate a little of the rice and a few pieces of fried tofu, until he realized it wasn't chicken. Neither of them was going to be any help at all.

Claire plastered on a smile and tried again. "But this food is really good."

"Well, I didn't make it. I ordered takeout."

"Oh." Claire's cheeks burned. She hadn't noticed any takeout containers. "Well. Um. It's good...uh, takeout."

Her aunt's lips twitched. "You're really trying, aren't you? And I am just giving you nothing."

Claire blinked. "Er," she said.

"Exactly." Aunt Jan managed to keep her face stern for another second, and then she snickered. It was the strangest sound, like a laugh and a whisper combined.

Claire and Patrick exchanged glances, and then they both started giggling, and a second later all of them were laughing. All of them except Claire's dad, who sat there looking confused.

Aunt Jan took one last shuddering breath, and then beamed at everyone. "Ah, that felt good. And Scottie, I'm still mad at you. But I shouldn't take it out on the kiddos. Kiddos, it's not your fault your dad's a ... well. Let's just say he's not my favorite person right now."

"Hey, that's something Claire says a lot," Patrick said.

"Does she? Intelligent girl, your sister."

Claire grinned. "Thanks."

"I *am* sorry, Jan," Claire's dad began.

Aunt Jan held up one hand and made a sharp slashing motion. "I don't want to hear it. Years. Years! You just stopped visiting. You stopped inviting *me* to visit. And all I got was the occasional phone call? A letter here or there? You know, I had to read about the plant shutting down in the papers! I didn't even know you'd lost your job until—" She stopped, her eyes narrowing.

Claire glanced at her dad. He wasn't looking at any of them, but instead fiddled with his fork.

"How bad did it get, Scottie?"

"It was fine."

"You didn't want my help. That's it, isn't it?"

"Can we maybe talk about this later?" he asked.

Aunt Jan nodded. "Oh, we'll talk." She made it sound like a threat.

"Does that mean you're staying mad at Dad?" Patrick asked.

"My sweet nephew, I'm always a little mad at your dad." She grinned. "But I got some satisfaction out of ordering

Thai food. He always hated anything with even the tiniest bit of spice. Such a baby."

Patrick winced.

"Oh, I'm sorry, honey. You don't like it, either?"

"It's just the tofu." Patrick wrinkled his nose. "It's like eating baked snot."

"Well, that's a horrifying image. Scratching tofu off my to-eat list for a while."

"Sorry," Patrick said. "The spice is okay, though."

Aunt Jan laughed. "Tomorrow I'll let you choose the restaurant. How's that?"

"Jan," Claire's dad said. "We're not staying long."

"Oh, nonsense. You can't wander around in a van forever, Scottie, and where else do you have to go? I mean, what with the house foreclo—"

"Jan!"

Claire froze. The house what? Her dad's face had gone pale, all except for two spots high on either cheek. Her aunt, by contrast, had gone almost as red as her hair.

"How do you even know about that?" he asked.

"It's called the internet, Scottie," Aunt Jan said. "I do try to keep tabs on you, you know."

"What are you talking about?" Claire asked. Her dad looked like he'd suddenly swallowed his tongue, silence falling thick and heavy across the table.

"You haven't told them?" Aunt Jan asked softly. "Oh, Scottie."

"Told us what?" Claire asked.

More silence.

"Told us *what*?" Claire demanded, slamming her hands against the table hard enough to make their dishes rattle. All her earlier frustration with her dad and his stories roared back through her veins. She *knew* he was keeping secrets. And she was tired of it.

"We'll talk about this later, honey," he said.

"No," Claire said. "I want to talk about it *now*."

"Claire—"

"Don't you trust us? Why won't you ever tell us anything true?" Tears pricked at the backs of her eyes, and she had to blink rapidly to keep them in. She didn't want to cry right now. She didn't want to be sad; she *wanted* to be angry.

Her dad massaged his neck, then sighed. "I didn't sell the house."

Claire caught her breath.

"I lost the house, okay? I'm not proud of it."

"You . . . lost the house?" Claire whispered.

"I couldn't make the mortgage payments. I . . . haven't been able to make them for a little while, actually, and finally the bank decided they'd waited long enough. So they took the house."

"That's why we left?" Patrick asked, his lower lip quivering. "It's not a Grand Adventure?"

"Oh, it's *definitely* a Grand Adventure." Their dad tried smiling. It was awful, and Claire looked down at her plate. "It's just . . . a well-timed adventure. I knew we'd have to move eventually, but moving is expensive and I wasn't sure where. So when Meredith called me about the van, I thought . . ." His shoulders slumped. "I thought it was the answer."

"It *is* the answer, Dad," Patrick said. "Even Claire likes it now."

"It's not really a permanent answer, though. Not with the two of you. I've been trying to find work along the way, but all of my contacts have been less than helpful."

"So, your friends we visited along the way . . ." Claire began.

"They were all people who, in the past, had said they'd help me get a job. But"—he shrugged—"so far it hasn't really panned out."

"But the van, Dad," Patrick tried again. "Hashtag vanlife—"

"Isn't going to work for us forever. I realized that once we met up with Celeste and her family. The last thing I want is to use the two of you like some kind of props to sell merchandise. That's not what us Jacobuses are about."

"Not all the vanlifers were like that," Patrick protested.

"Oh, true. But the others we met were all retired, or temporarily traveling. None of them had—" He stopped.

"Children," Claire finished for him. "None of them had children." A sudden image flashed through her mind, of Wrong Way Jacobus choosing his two calves over that fortune he'd been seeking, and suddenly everything clicked into place. Her dad was struggling to find work...because of them.

Claire had been so busy asking him why their mom had left, she'd never bothered to ask why *he'd* stayed.

"I was planning on telling you about the house later," he said.

"No, you weren't," Aunt Jan said. "This is how you are, Scottie. Anything you don't want to discuss gets conveniently glossed over."

"I knew coming here would be a mistake." He stood abruptly, his chair scraping against the floor.

"Scottie, wait."

But he strode from the room and out of the house, slamming the front door behind him.

Patrick turned wide eyes on Claire.

"It's okay," she said. "Dad just needs a little time to cool off."

"We're not going to California," Patrick whispered, and it wasn't a question. "We're not going to find Mom."

Now it was Claire's turn to hesitate, because this time the words didn't come to her.

But then her aunt spoke up. "Your mom?" She pursed her lips. "That woman was like a butterfly, always fluttering about. You're better off without her skipping in and out of your lives."

Patrick nodded slowly, moving his head up and down like he was eighty and not eight. "I'm going to go check on Dad. Just in case."

"You might want to wait a—" Aunt Jan began, but Patrick had already gotten up and sprinted outside. The front door slammed again. "Like father, like son, eh?"

Claire didn't know what to say to that, so she didn't say anything at all.

"I make you uncomfortable, don't I?" her aunt asked. At Claire's startled expression, she smiled. "I have that effect on people. It's because I don't like to waste time dancing around answers. Growing up, I always felt like your father did enough of that for the both of us."

"I . . . guess I can see that." Claire studied her aunt. "What happened, between you and Dad?" Claire tried to imagine a future where she and Patrick didn't see each other for several years. Sometimes she thought it would be nice to get a break from him. But, like, a week. Maybe a month . . . okay, two months, tops. But definitely not years. Just the thought made her heart ache. She'd lost enough people.

"I told your dad not to marry your mom."

Claire blinked.

"I told you, I don't like to dance around answers. Also it's late and I'm tired. But I think that's where the rift between us started. Obviously, he didn't listen to me."

Even though Claire never wanted to see her mother again, hearing this new information felt like getting smacked in the face with a bucket of cold water. "Why didn't you want him to marry her?"

Aunt Jan sighed. "I told him that Catherine was not the girl he imagined her to be. But you know your father. He builds up these elaborate stories, and then he starts to believe them."

For a second Claire was six years old again, and digging in her backyard. She'd been so excited to *look* for a spaceship, she hadn't cared about the dirt or the hot sun or the blisters. There was that surge of disappointment when she'd discovered the sewer, but mostly she remembered how much fun she'd had while digging, how she'd spent the time imagining where she'd go, which planets she'd see . . . In the end, the fact that she hadn't actually found a spaceship didn't really matter. It was only years later, when she looked back and realized how he'd made everything up, that she had gotten angry.

Maybe her dad's marriage to her mom was like that, full of magic at first, all fun, until the blisters started forming, and the fantasy wore off. Until all they had left was a dug-up sewer with no spaceship in sight.

"Anyhow, he was head over heels; there was no talking him out of it. He had some romantic little nickname for her and everything. And then, of course, your mom got pregnant with you, and that was the end of that."

Claire flinched.

"Oh, I'm sorry. I didn't mean that to sound so harsh. It's just . . . it's late. I wasn't expecting visitors today."

"Sorry about that."

Her aunt waved that away. "I'm glad you came. Truly." She took Claire's hands and squeezed them gently. "I've missed you. I've even missed Scottie. He's the most irritating person I've ever met, but he does make things more interesting."

Claire thought about that later as she brushed her teeth and took a long, long shower. And then she let the hot water push all her thoughts out of her head. As she got dressed in freshly washed pajamas and crawled under the covers of a real bed, she felt her whole body relaxing, and she fell asleep immediately.

Something woke her a few hours later. Maybe it was the emptiness of her room, or the quiet; she'd gotten used to road noises, the sound of her dad snoring, the creaking of the van in the wind. The house sounded a lot different, and her bed felt too flat, and she kind of missed the smell of diesel and wood.

Or maybe she was lonely.

Claire looked across the room at the other guest bed. It was empty. Patrick must have slept outside in the van with their dad. Claire pictured them both out there. *I'm comfortable. I'm warm. I can easily get up and use the bathroom in the middle of the night.* But these thoughts didn't help. Sighing, Claire kicked off her blankets and padded outside.

Her dad blinked at her when she opened the side door of the van. "Claire-bear?"

"Figured I'd join you and Patrick out here. Don't make fun of me." She looked above him. The hammocks weren't set up.

It felt like time slowed way down, until Claire was very aware of the space between each heartbeat. "Dad," she said carefully.

"Hrm?" he asked, still half asleep.

"Where's Patrick?"

He rubbed his eyes and yawned. "In the house, I'd guess."

"Didn't he come out here?"

"No." He sat up, his hand searching along the side of the van for the pocket where he kept his glasses. "I haven't seen him since I left the house. Why?"

Claire had a flash of insight. It was like the moment when she'd started telling Justin her story about the frogs, that second when the world had slammed into focus, everything brilliantly, blindingly clear. This felt the same, and she knew, in every fiber of her being, that Patrick wasn't in the house.

She sprinted inside and tore through all the rooms anyway, calling his name, but a few minutes later, she'd confirmed it.

Patrick was gone.

CHAPTER 30

Claire's dad kept his gaze focused on the road ahead as he drove, hands gripping the steering wheel so hard he was shaking. Or maybe that had nothing to do with his grip. "What if he's not on the train?" he asked.

"He's on the train," Claire said. "The California Zephyr. I'm sure of it." Her aunt had been making phone calls to the local authorities and beginning a search in the area, but when Claire told her dad where she thought Patrick had gone, he'd believed her. He'd believed her enough to hop in the van and start driving. Even if he was questioning it now.

"And you're sure he's going to your mom's place?"

"For the last time, Dad, yes. I'm sure. He thought we were going there on this trip, to rescue her. And when Aunt Jan told him we weren't . . ." Claire thought of her brother's face again, the slow nod. She should have known. She should have realized. It was a Tuesday, after all.

"Why on earth would he think *that*?"

Claire's stomach clenched, all the fear roiling inside her turning to hot, bubbling fury. "Why do you *think* he'd think that?" she practically spat. "Your stupid story!"

"My ... story?" He gaped, as if he'd never heard anything like this before. As if he had no idea. *No* idea!

Claire's anger wasn't boiling anymore; it was steaming, filling her vision with red and her ears with the pounding of her own too-fast heartbeat. "Wrong Way rescues Evangeline Rose, just like Patrick thought you were going to rescue Mom," she said bitterly. "Like you rescued her before, from the troll king. You *always* rescue her in your stories."

"Not true," her dad said quietly. "She rescues herself. I only ever *thought* she needed me to save her." He looked about a hundred years old, his shoulders slumped, face creased with worry.

Claire bit back her furious reply and actually considered his words, remembering how her mom had supposedly escaped the troll kingdom again when Claire was nine. How she'd gone on to become a pilot, a scientist, and a spy, before mimes trapped her. Before Claire stopped asking. And the last thing her dad had said about Evangeline Rose was that she could have left Dirk herself, if she'd wanted to. That she was strong enough to do anything, go anywhere.

Claire looked out the window. She didn't want to look at her dad anymore, at his sad, tired face. Instead, she focused on the mountains looming outside, their silhouettes cutting through the slowly lightening sky. Her mom didn't need to be rescued. She didn't *want* to be rescued. Her aunt's casual declaration swirled suddenly through Claire's mind: *And then, of course, your mom got pregnant with you, and that was the end of that.*

Her fault. She'd always known it, deep down. The real reason her mom had left. It wasn't because of her dad.

"Why couldn't you have just told us the truth?" she whispered, tears falling down her face faster than she could wipe them away. "If you'd just told us why Mom left, that she didn't w-want us ... If Patrick knew there was n-no hope ..."

"No hope?" her dad whispered. "I never wanted either of you to believe that."

Claire still couldn't look at him. "But if I ... if I hadn't been b-born," she managed, the words half a sob.

The van slowed, moved over to the shoulder of the road, and parked. "Claire, honey." Her dad unclipped his seatbelt and wrapped his arms around her, and just like she used to when she was a little kid, she cried all over the front of his ugly plaid shirt.

"Having you, and your brother, was the best thing that ever happened to me. I wouldn't trade it for anything. Not for all the gold in California." He stroked her hair. "And I never told you about your mother, because I could never think of a good way to explain what she did. *I* don't understand what she did. But know that when she left, she was leaving *me*. It had nothing to do with you or Patrick."

Claire thought of the frog again, the one that swallowed a rock. The one that might be dead now...or might be living in the pond, fully restored to health. If she chose to believe it.

She sniffed and pushed away from him. "We'd better hurry if we're going to get to Sacramento before Patrick." They'd peeled out of Aunt Jan's driveway around four that morning, and according to the train schedule, Patrick should be arriving a little after two in the afternoon. They should beat him there, but only just.

As long as he really *was* on that train.

Claire didn't let herself think about that. Her brother *had* to be on that train.

Her dad pulled back onto the highway, the only sound the tires rumbling over the road.

"Have you called Mom yet?" she asked.

Silence.

"Dad?"

"I probably should, huh?" He tapped the wheel. *Tap, tap, tap.* "Next rest area, I'll...I'll give her a call."

Claire was quiet for a long time after that, and so was her dad. But as the silence thickened, she had to ask. "Hey, Dad?"

"Hmm?"

"What *did* Evangeline Rose want? More than the chance at a new life?"

He shrugged. "Who can say?"

"You don't know?"

"I don't think even she knew, honey. I think that was the whole problem."

Claire curled up in her seat and watched the sky lighten into morning, and somewhere along the way, she fell asleep.

"He's not here. Dad, he's *not here!*" Claire had watched every single person getting off the train, and her brother had not been among them. What now? She'd been so sure.

"Scottie Jacobus?" A man stepped forward. His face was shadowed by a large hat, his eyes hidden behind aviator sunglasses, but his jaw was square and he walked like a man used to giving orders.

"Yes?" Claire's dad eyed him.

"I'm Derek Stone." He took off his sunglasses, his eyes hard and flat. "I have your son."

CHAPTER 31

Claire held her mug of tea in both hands but didn't drink any of it. Even if she liked tea, which she didn't, she wouldn't have been able to swallow anything around the lump in her throat.

She was sitting on a couch in the living room of her mother's condo, the one she'd glimpsed in that picture, watching the sky outside the window fade into the deep blue of a perfect California evening.

It smelled funny inside, the air full of dry heat. Her mom had a fireplace, one of those electric ones, and above it she'd hung an oil painting of a horse running through the surf. Claire didn't know her mother liked horses, but then, she didn't really know anything about what her mother liked. All she really knew, now that she was sitting here across from her, was that she'd rather be anywhere else.

Claire squeezed her mug, wishing it would shatter.

Patrick sat outside with their dad, getting the lecture of his life. Apparently Derek had caught up with the train one stop before, in Roseville, and being a cop, he'd been able to board and find Patrick skulking in one of the seats.

Also, apparently, Derek was engaged to their mother. Claire's dad hadn't seemed surprised when Derek told them that news, just like he hadn't been surprised when Derek admitted they still hadn't set an official date yet.

Claire hadn't said a word.

When they'd gotten to the condo, Patrick had bounded out to meet them, and even though Claire wanted to punch him, somehow she'd found herself hugging him so tight she could feel the air leave his lungs, hugging him as he gasped and squirmed until she let him go. But she still hadn't said a word.

All the words she hadn't said were now choking her, as she watched the woman who had been her mother, sitting on the loveseat across from her. She was still dyeing her hair a darker brown, like in the picture Claire and Ronnie had found, although it was longer now, curling down past her chin. She was skinnier, too, her arms more muscular. She probably did CrossFit or yoga or something like that. Maybe she and Derek did triathlons together on the weekend.

Claire's lips curled.

Her mom—Catherine—took a sip of her tea, then lowered her mug. Lipstick stained the rim. "So," she said. Like it was a complete sentence.

Claire said nothing.

"Aren't you going to talk to me? You must have questions."

Claire shrugged.

Catherine set her tea on the glass coffee table between them and leaned forward. "Claire, honey...I missed you."

"*Don't*." The word scraped from Claire's throat, raw and painful.

The woman in front of her flinched. "Look, I'm sorry—"

"No. You don't get to say that, either."

"Then what am I supposed to say? I *am* sorry, and I *did* miss you. Do you want me to lie to you?"

"I just want you to be quiet." Even Claire was surprised at how calm her words sounded. She realized, now, that she didn't need any answers from her mother. Her dad's stories might not have been real, but they had filled the hole inside where her mother used to be, and now she could look at her, and feel nothing. Her mother had made her choice, to walk away and not look back. And Claire had made her own choice years ago, to walk forward.

Catherine picked up her tea again, but didn't drink it. Instead, she stared down into the steam like it contained the winning lottery numbers. "I was so young when I met your father."

"You weren't *that* young."

"Nineteen might seem ancient to you, but trust me, it's really not. And twenty is very young to suddenly find yourself a mom. And your dad...we weren't a good match. It took me a long time to see the truth of it, because he'd paint this lovely story, and I'd fall into it and forget, and then the next thing I knew years had flown by and I was nowhere near where I wanted to be, and getting farther every day."

"So you left."

"I wasn't planning on leaving for good, just a short break. But the more time slipped past, the more I...I didn't think I'd be allowed to come back." Her face crumpled, but she took a slow, shaky breath, and kept it together. And Claire wondered if this was like her dad's tales, only this time it was a story her mom told herself. *I wanted to come back. I didn't think I could, but I wanted to.* "I wanted to call," her mom continued. "So many times. But I was afraid."

"Of what?"

She clutched her mug closer. "Of the silence, I guess," she whispered.

"I saw the divorce papers." And even though Claire felt nothing—*nothing*—she *wanted* to feel nothing, it was still hard to say, "And I saw that you didn't want any child custody."

Catherine looked away. "Having a baby seemed like such a Grand Adventure, and it was, but it took over everything. Some people..." She twisted her cup. "Some people just aren't cut out to be mothers. I thought it would be better for you, and Patrick, if I wasn't around." She looked up at the painting of the horse tearing wild and free through the surf, and a single tear trickled down from the corner of her eye. Claire silently watched its lonely progress until Catherine dashed it away. "Do you think you could ever forgive me?"

"I . . ." Claire's mind went blank. Forgive her? No. Never. But . . . "I don't know."

Catherine let out another shaky breath. "I guess that's still more than I deserve."

Neither of them spoke for several long moments. Catherine sipped her tea, the sound too loud in the stillness. Claire couldn't take it. "I do have another question," she said finally.

"Oh?"

"Dad's been telling us a story. A new one, not one he's told before. About one of our ancestors, and a woman named Evangeline Rose."

Her mom started so suddenly, she almost dropped her mug.

"So you know her," Claire said. It wasn't a question.

"Yes, I know her." Catherine's lips curved in a wry smile. "I *am* her. That's what my mom wanted to name me, but my dad convinced her to name me Catherine instead. Much more practical. When I told that to your father . . . I think it was even before we started dating? He was so taken with that name, he called me Evangeline Rose for the next

month." She laughed. "I haven't heard that name in years..."
The laughter faded. "Years," she repeated.

"What about Edgar? Wrong Way Jacobus?"

Catherine shook her head. "Your dad probably made him up."

"But if Evangeline is—"

"You know your dad, he was never very good at separating fact from fiction."

Fact and fiction. Her mom had made up an entirely new life, a life where she pretended she didn't have kids at all. So maybe she wasn't very good at it, either. Claire looked at that horse painting again over the fireplace, and this time she noticed the signature at the bottom, the large looping "C" written in the same style Claire used.

Maybe the line between fact and fiction was more of a blurry squiggle, and no one was good at separating them.

Claire's head spun, and she knew she had to leave. She couldn't stay here a second longer.

The front door opened, and Patrick stuck his head in. "Mom?"

"Come here, sweetie." She opened her arms wide.

Claire's heart twisted as her brother picked his way across the spotless condo and hesitated. He didn't hug Catherine but instead perched next to her on the loveseat, still moving in that weird, self-conscious way. Claire knew he was hoping for a fairy tale, just as she knew he'd never find it here.

Stories don't always end the way we'd hope.

"Hey, Patrick?" Claire said.

Her brother looked up, eyes wide.

"I'm going out to the van."

"Don't be silly," Catherine said. "I have a guest bedroom, and—"

"I'm going out to the van," Claire repeated. "Come on out when you want to, okay?"

He nodded.

"You okay here now?"

He nodded again.

Claire let her eyes shift to the side, to Catherine. She stood without saying anything, but then, just before she slipped outside, she whispered, "Good night, Mom," because maybe she wanted to pretend a little, too.

"Claire?"

Claire opened her eyes. The inside of the van was dark, but she could make out a Patrick-sized silhouette in front of her. "Hmm?" she said.

"Just checking to see if you're still awake."

"I was asleep."

"I know. But now you're not." He climbed up into his hammock.

"Dad go inside?" Claire asked.

"Yeah. He's ... talking."

Talking. To his ex-wife and her soon-to-be second husband. That would be more uncomfortable than watching her dad thumb dance in public, and Claire was glad she was missing it.

"Claire?"

"Yeah?"

"Can you ... can you tell me a story?"

"Me?" She blinked, surprised. "You want a story from me?"

"Yeah. Only not a frog story. Not when I'm sleeping in a hammock."

She chuckled. "What kind of story, then?"

"How about a troll story? Like the kind Dad used to tell us when we were little."

"You're still little."

"I'm not that little." Patrick shifted, his hammock creaking as he turned toward her. "Please?"

"Fine," Claire said. A troll story. She coughed, suddenly self-conscious. The only story she'd ever told had flown out of her in a tide of rage. But she didn't feel angry right now. She felt ...

Sad.

Claire closed her eyes and let herself feel that. She thought of her mother, who wanted forgiveness, but not a place in their lives, who painted horses running through oceans, but had saddled her own life to a Dirk Rockaford. Then she thought of her dad's Wrong Way Jacobus and his search for Evangeline Rose, and how somewhere along the way that quest became less important than caring for his cows. And finally, she thought of Patrick, who'd been hoping for some kind of story of his own, a story with a fairy-tale ending, and instead was left with . . . what?

She cleared her throat. "Once upon a time—"

"Seriously?"

"Hey, you asked me to tell you a story, so I'm telling you a story. Which means I get to choose how it begins. And this one begins, 'Once upon a time.' You got that?"

"Fine," Patrick grumbled.

"Once upon a time," Claire said firmly, "there was a queen. She was beautiful, so beautiful, with eyes the color of moss and skin that glowed like the reflection of the moon on water."

"She's not a frog queen, is she?"

"No, she's not a frog queen."

"Because you said you weren't going to bring up frogs, and here you're all talking about water and moss and—"

"She's not a frog queen! She's a troll queen, okay?"

"I guess that's okay."

Claire sighed. "This troll queen had everything she could possibly desire, but still, she couldn't be satisfied. She wanted a larger cave, so her husband, who adored her, built a new cave with his bare hands. She wanted more gems, so her daughter, who adored her, emptied all of her treasure chests at the queen's feet, until the entire cave floor glittered with them. And still she wanted more...

"Her son, who adored her most of all, asked what he could bring her. As this was 'once upon a time,' he knew his mother just needed a third task completed, and her curse of restlessness would be broken.

"'I don't know what I want,' she told him, again and again. 'I just know that I want.' And then one night, one clear summer night, she went out to the little pool outside her enormous cave and sat beside it. And this time she noticed the reflection of the moon, and how it glowed even more brightly than she ever could. And suddenly she knew exactly what she wanted.

"'Son,' she called. 'Fetch me the moon, and then I shall be happy.'

"Her son looked at her with his large troll eyes, and then looked at the moon, so far away. It seemed impossible. 'If I do this for you, will you be satisfied?'

"His mother nodded, for she was sure this was all that she was lacking.

"'Then I will find a way.' He thought about it all the rest of that night and all the next day. His sister, who adored him, found him wandering their cave, crying crystal troll tears.

"'What is wrong, dear brother?'

"'I don't know how to reach the moon.'

"'The moon?' His sister wiped his face and smiled. 'That's easy. We just need to find a spaceship.'

"'And where can we possibly find one of those?'

"She thought about it, all that next night and all the next day. Her father, who adored her, found her hunched in the corner of their cave, pulling on the strands of her moss hair in frustration.

"'What is wrong, dear daughter?'

"'I don't know how to find a spaceship.'

"'And why do you need a spaceship?' he asked, gently lifting her hands from her hair and pulling her to her feet.

"'So my brother and I can reach the moon.'

"'And why must you reach the moon?'

"'So we can catch it and bring it to our mother. So that she will finally be happy.'

"'Well, I do know where a spaceship is buried,' her father said. 'And if you ask me to, I will fly it to the moon with you and your brother. I will do anything that you ask me to do, for such is my love for you both. But know this: when someone asks for the moon, it's never just the moon.'"

Claire stopped talking, her throat raw.

"What happened next?" Patrick whispered.

She swallowed and opened her eyes. "They flew to the moon, of course, and working together, the three of them trapped it and brought it down into the cave for the queen."

"And … was she happy?"

"She was," Claire admitted. "All that night and the day after, she was happy. But then as the next night began, she noticed how dark it was outside. How gloomy. And she sat there by her pool until the sun came up. The beautiful, glorious sun. A single crystal tear slid down her cheek, and she knew, if she could just have that sun, *then* she'd be happy."

Patrick was so still in the dim van for so long that Claire wondered if he'd gone to sleep. And then he let out a breath that might have been a sob.

Claire reached across the five inches of space between them, so much space, and tousled his hair. "Good night," she said. "I love you, you know that?"

"Yeah," he mumbled, fixing his hair. "I know."

Claire was almost asleep when she heard him say, "I love you, too." She smiled, until he added, "I liked your frog story better, though."

CHAPTER 32

The next day, Claire woke up early. Her dad was snoring below her, her brother sleeping with one arm thrown across his face. Claire pulled a blank postcard out from the front zippered pocket of her backpack and drew a picture. Then she wrote her mother a note beside it.

She didn't forgive her. She'd probably never forgive her. But at least now a part of her understood her.

Claire slipped out of bed.

"Ow, Claire," her brother whined.

"Shh," she said, accidentally stepping on her dad's head.

"Ow, Claire," he groaned. "You've made your point, okay? Next time I'll build you a stupid toilet."

"And shower?"

"Don't push your luck." He sat up, reaching for his glasses. "Guess I'm awake now."

"I'm just dropping something off," Claire said quickly. She wasn't ready to share it, not with anyone else.

Her dad smiled. "Go drop it off, and we'll hit the road, okay? Sound good, Patrick?"

"Can we get waffles?"

"Sure. We can get waffles."

"Then it sounds good."

"What do you folks want to do next?" their dad asked as they sat in the diner, eating their breakfast.

"We could go visit Julian again," Patrick suggested. "Maybe he has more tips for me."

"Absolutely not!" Their dad's jaw clenched. It turned out Julian's advice for how to slip into a place unnoticed worked as well for a train as it did for an amusement park. Patrick said he had snuck past the conductor by pretending he was hurrying after his mom, and then spent the train ride in what he described as a "vicious cat and mouse game" with that same conductor. Later, he admitted that they'd actually only gone around checking tickets once, which he'd avoided by crouching among the luggage by the doors.

"Maybe we could go back to Aunt Jan's," Claire suggested carefully. "I think ... I think she'd like that."

"You do?" Her dad sounded surprised.

"I think she's lonely."

He seemed to consider that. "I do owe her a few years' worth of visits, I suppose. And she did say we could come by anytime."

"And stay as long as we wanted," Patrick said. "Unless she's mad at me now?"

"I'm pretty sure we're all mad at you," their dad said.

"Can you really be mad at *this*?" Patrick beamed his widest, brightest smile, and pointed at it.

Their dad shook his head. "I can't believe I'm feeding you waffles."

"You trained him," Claire said. "Well... you and Julian."

Her dad chuckled, and Claire wondered if the Great Train Adventure would work its way into his next round of stories, becoming a part of Patrick's legend. And someday, maybe Patrick's great-great-great-grandkids would hear some version of it.

"What about the rest of the story?" Patrick asked suddenly. "After Wrong Way rescued Evangeline Rose and brought her to Michigan, what happened? Did she leave?"

Claire frowned out the window. The sky was already hazy with the start of the day's heat, but the diner was nice and cool. Outside she could see a few cars lined up in the parking lot, but if she squinted, she could see the reflection of her own face instead, and her brother's face. And her dad's.

He was watching her and Patrick, that same fragile expression filling his eyes and deepening the lines of his face. Like he was bracing himself for bad news. "Yes," he said finally. "She left."

Patrick considered this. "So...Wrong Way ended up alone?"

"He wasn't alone," Claire said abruptly, turning back to the table. "Wrong Way had Sourdough. And he had Rye." She smiled at her dad. "And that was all the family he'd ever need."

Tears filled her dad's eyes and spilled over his cheeks, and he let them. And even though he was crying, Claire thought he looked happier than she'd ever seen him.

Finally he scrubbed his arm across his eyes, then beamed at her and Patrick. "Let's go home." And they left the diner and went back to their van.

Epilogue

H ow do I look?"

Claire looked her dad up and down. "Like a museum attendant."

He grinned. "But a fun one, right?"

"As fun as one could possibly be," she muttered.

"I suppose that's the best praise I'll get. I'll see you in a few hours. If all goes well, I'll take you and your brother out for a celebratory ice cream. And if it doesn't go well? I'll make your aunt take us all out for a commiseratory ice cream instead."

"Pretty sure that's not a word, Dad," Claire said.

"Well, it should be." He checked his phone. "Ack! Gotta run."

Claire lay on her bed in her aunt's guest room and stared up at the ceiling. They'd been there for a little over a week, and it was starting to feel almost like home. Although secretly Claire kind of missed her hammock in the van, the feel of the diesel engine rumbling, the knowledge that they might go anywhere. But the future was an open road, and even though they had moved in with her aunt Jan for the next school year, the summer afterward was wide open.

Claire's fingers ached, and she looked down, surprised to see her hands curled into fists.

"Your dad leave for his job interview?" her aunt asked from the doorway.

"Yeah." Claire shook out her fingers, and as they unfurled, she knew what she had to do. "Can I borrow your phone?"

A few minutes later and Claire had dialed Ronnie's number by heart. Her mom had never called them because she was scared of the silence. Claire didn't want to be like that.

Besides, if she never called, then silence was all she *would* get.

"Hello?" Ronnie's deep, confident voice filled the phone.

"H-hey," Claire said, suddenly shy.

"Claire? Claire! I'm so glad you're not dead!"

"Why would I be dead?"

"You stopped writing me! And your dad never answered his phone, even though I tried calling it a hundred times. Mike was all set to track you down."

"You tried calling?"

"Obviously!"

Claire frowned. "But ... Oh."

"Oh? Oh?"

Her dad had bought a new phone right before they'd left. He must have gotten a new number, too. "I forgot," Claire whispered, embarrassment flooding through every inch of her.

"You forgot what? What's going on? What are you up to out there? How's hashtag vanlife?"

"Whoa," Claire said. "Slow down a little, Ronnie. Give yourself some space."

Silence. Then, "That's not funny."

Claire laughed. "It's a little funny."

Click-click. Click-click.

Claire's heart stuttered, just for a second. "H-hi, Mike."

"H-hey Claire," he stammered back.

Claire tried to think of something else to say, but her mouth had gone strangely dry and no words escaped.

"Well, this got awkward quickly," Ronnie said, and Claire could practically hear her smirking. "But that's not surprising. Nothing more awkward than puppy love."

"Ronnie!" Claire and Mike both protested.

Ronnie chuckled. "See? Totally awkward."

"Whatever," Claire said, but she found herself smiling.

"So tell us," Ronnie said. "What's the vagabond lifestyle been like?"

Warmth filled Claire's chest as she cradled the phone against her ear. "Ah," she began. "Now, that is an interesting story."

Author's Note

The very first time I remember thinking about money was soon after my dad lost his job. I was around eight or nine, close to the age Patrick is in *Wrong Way Summer*, and my parents tried to act as if everything was the same, even as they began screening phone calls and fighting with each other more often. I can still recall the many voicemail messages from creditors cluttering up our answering machine, how they seemed to seep out into the air itself.

My mom assured me we were "getting by." And we were. We weren't in danger of going hungry or losing our house. There were plenty of others who had it way worse. Now that I'd gotten my first glimpse at money troubles, I noticed how other families carried around the same familiar tension. And while eventually my dad found another job and things went slowly back to normal for my family, I'll never forget the stress of waiting for the answering machine to pick up, or of listening to my parents argue that very particular kind of fight that was less about anger and more about fear.

Fast-forward many years, and I found myself living in Santa Cruz, California, a place with excellent weather, gorgeous beaches, and a truly astronomical cost of living. We used to joke that in Santa Cruz, everyone has three jobs: the job that pays the bills, the "passion" job, and the other job that pays the bills. And still, sometimes, that wasn't enough. According to the 2017 Santa Cruz County Point-in-Time Census, approximately one out of every 120 people in the area is homeless; many of them either currently employed or actively looking for work. And a lot of the people defined as homeless are living out of their vehicles.

If you look up #vanlife on Instagram, you'll see plenty of beautiful photographs of people converting their vans into tiny homes and traveling around the country and the world. You'll see lovely beaches and artfully posed couples and read about adventure and travel lust and escape. When I first heard about #vanlife, I was definitely swept up in the romanticism of it all. My husband and I already owned a van—courtesy of our dog walking business—and all we'd have to do would be to convert it and take off.

But then I began noticing all the people living in their less glamorous vehicles, right there in my town. I talked to a fellow dog walker who admitted he'd lived in his car for three months after his landlord raised the rent too high and he couldn't immediately find another affordable place that would accept his dog. I heard from students who couldn't find housing—there isn't enough on campus, and many off-campus landlords don't want to rent to large groups of students. I met a woman who chose to live in her truck camper so she could work just one job and then have the time to pursue the things she cared about, the things that had brought her to the area in the first place.

That's when I realized that so many more people than I had ever thought were just "getting by." Some people willingly chose #vanlife, and some came to embrace it, but for many people it was a beautiful story told to make the best of a tough situation. In our society, we trade hours of our lives away for money. Sometimes people weren't willing, or able, to trade enough away to afford housing.

I did end up trying the vanlife myself, and it is a mixture of romantic and wonderful—adventure! escape! wanderlust!—and stressful. The constant worry about making rent is replaced by a new worry over where to park the van for the night. Showering and other basic human necessities become issues to plan ahead for and strategize around. Still, much like my characters at the beginning of *Wrong Way Summer*, I felt like I was on a Grand Adventure. But unlike them, I knew how this adventure would end: I had a place waiting for me when I was done exploring life on the road. And that is a luxury that many of the people I met did not have.

I thought a lot about that luxury when I sat down to write *Wrong Way Summer*. Like my own dad, the dad in this story loses his job. But unlike my dad, this father is never able to recover financially, and instead ends up losing the house. He uses the #vanlife narrative of "houselessness as an exciting choice" in order to protect his kids from the scary realities of their situation. And like any story, it's not really a lie, but instead a way of getting at a deeper truth: No matter how secure a person feels, it only takes one crisis—a health problem, a lost job, a new landlord—to potentially change everything. And when that happens, sometimes the ability to choose the narrative is the only real choice we have.

Acknowledgments

As always, so many people helped this story become a book, and I'm grateful to each and every one of them, including my amazing and supportive agent, Jennifer Azantian; my fantastic, eagle-eyed editor, Erica Finkel; and everyone else at Abrams, especially Siobhán Gallagher, Amy Vreeland, Emily Daluga, Jenn Jimenez, Brooke Shearouse, Nicole Schaefer, Trish McNamara O'Neill, Jenny Choy, Andrew Smith, Jody Mosley, Melanie Chang, Elisa Gonzalez, Mary Wowk, and Michael Jacobs.

I'm very fortunate in all my writer friends, but this book especially owes a lot to Justin Stewart, who read my opening and encouraged me to keep going, Suzi Guina, who talked me through a plot tangle or two, and the rest of my Kidliterati group: Katie Nelson, Tara Creel, Kaitlin Hundscheid, and Jennifer Camiccia. My support crew for this book also included my cousin Kitty, who shared words of encouragement (and wine) when I needed them most.

I first heard the saying "Never let the facts get in the way of a good story" from my late Grandpap Crowley. I hope he would be proud of how I've put that motto to use. I also borrowed the last name and larger-than-life charisma (and epic thumb dancing!) from my late uncle Bill, who I didn't really get a chance to know, but whose stories have taken on a life of their own. Thank you to the rest of the Jacobus family for welcoming me and sharing those stories, especially my mother-in-law Lyn Lang, who also shared the legend of her ancestor "Wrong Way Jacobus," and allowed me to invent my own version.

I shamelessly borrowed troll tales and mannerisms from my uncle Steve, as well as certain personality traits from my cousins, Christy and Paul. Thank you for keeping my childhood summers exciting. Also thank you to Aunt Chris for keeping an eye on all of us. And to the rest of my family, including my parents, Rich and Rose, my in-laws, Lyn and Bruce, my sisters, Kati, Rosi, and Ashley, and my brothers, Ed, Nick, and Jesse: I would not be the person I am today without all of you in my life.

And finally, to my husband Sean. There is no one I'd rather share a van with. Thank you for all the adventures.

About the Author

Heidi Lang believes that the next Grand Adventure is always just around the corner. She has chased her love of judo from the East to the West Coast, run ultramarathons, started her own dog walking business, and converted a Sprinter van into a tiny home so she could experience #vanlife. Currently she lives in eastern Washington with her husband and two dogs. She is the coauthor of The Mystic Cooking Chronicles series (*A Dash of Dragon*, *A Hint of Hydra*, and *A Pinch of Phoenix*), as well as the author of *Rules of the Ruff*.